The Stone Thrower

by
Adam Marek

About the Author

Adam Marek is an award-winning short story writer. He won the 2011 Arts Foundation Short Story Fellowship, and was shortlisted for the inaugural Sunday Times EFG Short Story Award. His first story collection *Instruction Manual for Swallowing* was longlisted for the Frank O'Connor Prize. His stories have appeared in many magazines, including *Prospect* and *The Sunday Times Magazine*, *The Stinging Fly*, *The London Magazine* and *Riptide*, and in many anthologies including *Lemistry, Litmus, The New Uncanny* and *Bio-Punk* from Comma Press, The British Council's *New Writing 15*, and *The Best British Short Stories 2011*.

Visit Adam Marek online at **www.adammarek.co.uk**

Contents

Fewer Things 1
Dead Fish 9
Tamagotchi 17
Without a Shell 31
The Stone Thrower 43
Remember the Bride who got Stung? 49
An Industrial Evolution 61
The Captain 79
A Thousand Seams 97
The Stormchasers 111
Santa Carla Day 117
Burying Chiyoko Sasaki 133
Earthquakes 149

Acknowledgements 168

Fewer Things

WE GO DOWN to the beach at dawn to stop the chicks from choking. I put on jeans and a heavy jumper over my pyjamas. My pee steams in the cold bathroom. Dad shakes the house awake with his footsteps. Time to go, he says with one finger in his ear.

My face shrinks in the cold outside. I lost a glove yesterday, so this bare hand goes deep into my pocket, among the snotty tissues and the fossils. There are new flowers on the cliff top. Dad brushes them with the sole of his boot. I'm not sure what he's checking, but he seems pleased.

Ours are the only footprints on the sandy slope. I once fell here, years ago, and sliced my face on the grass, which grows in tufts like buried pincushions. The scar has faded to silver on my cheek. It is the shape of a bird's footprint.

Dad does his long-legged run, and I keep back from the sand he kicks up behind him. He has already seen a tern chick, on the beach at the bottom of the cliff. At first, the fish stuck in its throat looks like a long tongue. The chick is flicking its head to the side, then lunging forward, gagging. It takes a few steps, stumbles under the weight of the fish, then quickly rights itself.

We have to do this at dawn, and we have to be fast, because we're racing against the gulls and the skuas that wake up desperate with hunger.

Dad chases the little ball of fluff across the sand, then takes it up in his fingers, clamping its tiny head with one hand while gently pulling out the fish with the other. The chick struggles, pushing its grey webbed feet against his palms. He mumbles to the chick, soft sounds that are more like thoughts than words.

The knuckle-fish hasn't gone too far down this chick's throat. If the fish goes all the way down, the two barbs on its back hook inside the bird's neck and it can't be pulled out without tearing open the chick's throat. There is only one thing that Dad can do with the birds when this happens. He makes the decision quickly, and without speaking. They are so fragile, it takes just a small tug, and then Dad slips them into his bag.

I turn my shoulder against the freezing wind blowing in off the sea. Dad slides the fish out of the chick's beak. It's a smooth movement, and at the end of it, when the trumpet-shaped head of the fish comes out, I actually feel relief myself. As if the fish had been stuck in my throat.

He wants me to be able to do this myself. One day, he says, if there are any of them left, this will be your job. I wonder if there are other people like us, on other islands, going through this same strange routine, but if they exist, they are too far away for me to sense them. Sometimes it feels like we're not just the only people on the island, it feels like we're the only people on the planet.

The dead fish goes in Dad's bag – he doesn't chuck it in case the chick tries to eat it again. He takes the fish back to the house to weigh and measure and record on his laptop. I help him with this too. It's odd when this little event gets turned into numbers and dates, and then sent off somewhere to be analysed. They don't record any of the things that I remember: the way the chick's eyes widen as the fish starts to back out of its throat, the smell of Dad's bag, or the sound of the chick's feet as it skips across the sand.

We find three more that morning. When we're done, my stomach is so empty that if I open my mouth, I can hear the sound of the waves echoing inside it.

Porridge thickens in the pan while Dad lays out the four knuckle-fish on a week-old newspaper. Knuckle-fish are long and bony, a grotesque musical instrument you'd never put to your lips. Their fins are spiky fans. Even if the chicks could swallow these fish, they would give no nourishment.

When you're starving, Dad says, you'll eat anything that looks like food.

The birds are really after sandeels, the fat silver fish that are all meat. But the sandeels have vanished, and so too have the tiny plankton that they eat.

I spoon honey into the porridge while Dad measures the fish with a metal ruler. I wonder why parent birds feed chicks with fish that will kill them. It would be like Dad pouring petrol into my breakfast.

Later, we're out on the grassy clifftop overlooking the bay. I check my mobile again, even though I know the island gets no signal, just in case. Maybe Mum has left a message for us, for me, and it's out there, on the mainland, waiting.

The postman comes every three days if the waves are not too big for his small boat. I wonder about asking him to take the phone with him, so that it can fish in the air for messages and then bring them back to me.

What have you got there? Dad asks.

I stash the phone into my pocket. Nothing, I say.

Dad has his arm down a rabbit hole, all the way up to his shoulder. His feet kick the grass for balance while he probes the hole with his hand. He makes a disappointed grunt as he pulls his arm out. I draw a cross on the map, as I have been shown. Last year there was a tick here. We've had the same thing all day.

The first year Dad brought me here, every burrow had a puffin nest. I was too young to hold the map then, so Dad did everything, marking the positions, putting each chick into a cloth bag so it didn't get scared while he weighed it, and then clamping a flat ring around its leg, so he'd recognise it if he saw it again.

I wonder where all of those rings are now. Maybe somewhere far out there's a big whirlpool that's sucking everything in, all the birds and the fish and the phone calls, taking them down to the bottom of the ocean, to another world.

Late in the afternoon, we see two big skuas squabbling over a guillemot chick. They jab at it with their beaks, which are thick and dark, like medieval weapons. The chick is tiny next to their bulk. It stares out to sea, as if they might go away if it pretends they aren't there.

I start to run at them. I can get there in time to scare the skuas off, but Dad's arm bars my way. It's supposed to be like this, he says. We don't rescue worms from robins.

But, I say, why do we save the chicks that are choking and not this one?

Because the knuckle-fish are our fault, he says.

The skua with the streaky feathers, the one that looks older, made mean by years of scavenging icy oceans, snatches the chick from the beak of the younger one. It flicks its head back, and with a guzzling movement, swallows the chick down whole.

Where there were three living things, there are now two. Nothing exists of the chick except in my memory.

I make dinner. Spaghetti with cheese sauce out of a packet. There is an old square tin of mustard at the back of the cupboard, and I chip at the caked yellow powder until a few lumps are free. I tip these into the sauce, turning the steam poisonous for a second.

Dad is on the sofa ignoring the TV. His socks stink and are up on the table. He is massaging his eyebrows, which are so thick they bristle against his fingernails.

I imagine whacking him on the back of his head with the saucepan. The cheese sauce dribbling over his face. I imagine punching him in the mouth. I imagine it so hard I can feel the shape of his teeth on my fist.

Packet mixes, feet on the table. These are things that would not exist if Mum were here.

When I go to bed, I leave the dirty plates in the sink. Dad hasn't moved.

At night, the storm petrels keep me awake. They nest deep in the old castle ruins. For centuries, people thought that this island was haunted because of their dreadful wailing. They only come out at night, small and bat-like, draping terror over the cliff tops.

Dad says that it's probably the superstitions about the island that make it such a perfect place for wildlife. The locals left it alone, and did not raid it for eggs and feathers and meat, as they did other islands.

Even though I know the sound is made by birds, I struggle to think happy thoughts.

It's barely light and we are already out, taking long steps across the top of the rocks that are still wet from the tide. I see a tern chick, just standing still on a rock with a knuckle-fish in its throat, looking up at the sky. Maybe it's waiting for the parent that fed it the fish to come and pluck it out again.

You get that one, Dad says, and climbs down towards another chick he has seen on the beach.

Me? I say, but he has already gone.

I take my time climbing up, being more careful than I need to. I want Dad to finish quickly and to come and deal with this one. But even though I'm moving like a tortoise, he hasn't finished with the other chick by the time I reach mine.

What should I do? I call out. The chick flinches at my voice. I can see the grey of its skin beneath its fluff. I've never looked so closely.

Just pull it out, Dad calls up. He is irritated. Maybe there is something awkward about his bird.

I move my hands slowly, half hoping the chick will run away from me, but it does not. I've seen this done hundreds of times. My fingers seem to know how to catch and clutch the chick all by themselves. They have been learning while I watched. The tern is small and bony under its fluff. How could its parent have thought it could eat this huge fish? The knuckle-fish is stretching the bird's mouth wide. I wonder how far down it goes. Maybe its snout is deep inside the chick's belly.

I try to mumble to the chick, the way that Dad does, but I do not know its language. With the heel of my hand, I hold it on my knee, clamping its head with my fingers. I take one last look around. Dad is still with the other one.

The knuckle-fish's tail is cold and rough in my fingertips. I start to pull. The chick's whole head comes forward, and it makes a noise of alarm. I look again at the fish, and my blood turns to saltwater.

I think it's stuck, I call out.

Well do it quickly, he says.

But it's stuck!

Do it like I showed you.

I want you to do it.

Just do it.

A big gull wheels round the head of the cliff, then balances on the breeze, gripping the sky with its wingtips right above me. Its shrieks are prehistoric.

Dad, I say, the barbs are stuck. I don't think he has understood.

One quick... he says, and makes a gesture with his hands – his two fists together, then snapped apart. I've seen him do it enough times. There is no question. This is what he expects of me.

Can you come and do it?

It's suffering while you're whining, he says.

Dad's chick is now free and has run for cover.

I try once more to slide the fish out, and the chick squeaks as the barbs tug inside its throat. My heart is thumping. Dad is standing at the bottom of the cliff with his hands on his hips.

I just hold the chick, its head in one hand, its feet in the other. I hope that my hands will do it themselves, that they will end the bird the same way they caught it, without me thinking about it. But my hands are waiting for instruction. I just sit on the wet rock, refusing to move, the wind curling under my hood.

And then Dad is there, right behind me. For goodness' sake, he says. He takes the bird's feet from my hand. Don't let go, he tells me. I tighten my grip on the bird's head and it's hard to hold on to as he tugs its feet. One hard yank, and it's over before I really understand what is happening.

Dad holds open his bag. Put it in, he says.

The bird has shrunk in my fingers. I lay it at the bottom of the bag, and my hand comes out smelling miserable.

Let's move on, Dad says.

The empty space we leave on the cliff is like the sound a door makes after it is shut.

At Christmas, when I was little, we used to play a game where Mum would remove one object from the living room while I was outside. When I came back in, I would always spot the empty space, no matter how small, within seconds. Even though I could never have named all the objects in the room, I was an expert at spotting the space left by something when it was gone.

Dad does not remember this game. You have a funny brain, he says. His mind is a pocket with a hole in the bottom.

I want to go home now. But I know that one of these empty spaces is there waiting for me. The one thing that made all of this bearable is not there.

My boots creak in the cold as I stand up. I check my phone one more time, but there are no messages. Dad starts down the cliff, back towards the path, and I follow.

Dead Fish

HERE COME THE pounding footfalls of a boy on the run. Alongside the canal, where algae strangle a neglected bicycle, Rupi appears, skinny as wicker. If you could slow this moment down, you'd see in his shoes all the places where the leather has broken away from the sole, and these holes opening and closing every time his foot hits the pavement, showing us his pale toes cowered together.

Rupi takes the stairs to the bridge two at a time. We are close enough to smell the stolen trout stuffed inside his jacket.

And here come his pursuers. Hear their shouts ringing against the bare bulbs strung in chains along the canal, shaking the sleeping filaments. At the bottom of the canal, an army of crayfish shudders beneath their reflections.

Let's move up, above the rooftops, where moss silences chimneys. From here we can see the boy weaving through a tangle of cobbled alleyways, his feet kicking up puffs of fungus spores.

The policemen are a little way behind and have lost him. They stop and pant, confronted with three empty passageways. One of them cups his hands behind his ears, making a radar antenna of his head. He swivels back and forth.

Before they find Rupi again, come with me quickly to the place where this chase began.

In the marketplace the weed-cutters work the stones with hoes, scraping up great heaps of tangled Grinch hair. Notice how smartly everyone is dressed, as if elegance could ward off the rot. The pockets of their coats are nurseries where the lint grows roots.

We can move through the crowds without anyone bumping us with their elbows. Let's go under the canopies where the soup steam gathers. Where sellers call out their wares. To the fishmonger's stall. His buckets are heaped with samphire. Fish glisten beneath the ice. The theft of one fish might not seem worthy of such a fearsome pursuit, but these fish are special.

No fish like this live anywhere near here any more. In all of the rivers and out at sea, fishermen's lines have hung dead for decades. And the people have no taste for the muddy crayfish that eat every other living thing in the rivers and canals. These fish had to be brought from far away, and distances are so much further than they used to be.

Braughin, the fishmonger, is one of five brothers who cut out into the barren sea with an almost supernatural sense of where the little pockets of fish remain. Their skill is unique, and so they can afford to charge four days' wages for a single fish. At dinner parties, these fish are status symbols for people such as the lady next to us, Alice, who reeks of lavender.

Tonight, Alice and her husband are entertaining the headmaster of St Nathan's, desperately hoping that their son will get a place there five years from now when he is old enough. The alternative schools are unthinkable.

Each of her decisions about the evening has been a source of worry. So much depends upon it. The education ladder here is climbed with knives and forks. Last year her sister slipped on just such an ascent, and tumbled all the way down to John Hopworth's.

When people talk about John Hopworth's, they talk about the history teacher who was burned alive in a toilet cubicle, about the seven teachers who have fled the school on their first day after being 'balded' by their students. Balding is a John Hopworth's welcome for new teachers. The students wrestle the teachers to the floor, pin them down with their knees, and cut their hair as close to the skin as the safety scissors can get. Alice's sister was so ruined by her daughter's experiences at John Hopworth's that they no longer share a family resemblance.

Slide with me down the seam of Alice's long jacket, along her bare leg. We've no time for her lovely knee. Skip straight over her ankle to her blister-red shoes. Notice how the tall thin heel of her right shoe bows and will soon break. Time and nature corrupt everything here.

But we cannot wait right now to see this woman topple, even though we lick our lips at the prospect, because Rupi's hounds have found him again.

Rupi's pace has slowed. There is not enough meat on his bones to sustain such a flight. His broken shoes flap hard against the cobbles. Now he scarpers past the bio-power station. The sound of slurry crashing into the river drowns the footsteps of his pursuers. For a moment he thinks they are gone, but he dare not look back.

Here are the steps down. Watch Rupi's practised slide on the algae-slicked rail. He hits the ground running, his fingers stretched out as if the air were a substance he must claw his way through. Tucked inside his jacket, the fish nods encouragement.

Indulge me for a second as we linger at an apartment window too greened up for anyone else to see the couple inside. Their sweaty limbs slap together, antagonizing the dust mites. Morris tells Danya that he can't hold on much longer. The mildew in his lungs makes his voice rattle. He grits his teeth and the dust mites grumble.

But we mustn't let Rupi get away from us. Back with him, we see over his shoulder that the policemen are gaining. They are sweating in their jackets. Their silver buttons tremble against their chests. They no longer call out, saving their breath for the pursuit.

Not one of these men will stop and show himself a weakling to the other two. They no longer care about the fish. They only care about beating the thief. In fact, look now, the one in front licking the spit from his lips already has his stick in his fist.

While we have been watching them, they have closed more distance on Rupi, as if our attention has sped them along. Let us blow at the boy's heels, become breathless ourselves.

Time now to overtake Rupi. The city around us blurs. If only he could move so quickly. We zip ahead to Rupi's home. Over the canal and hidden people waiting, over the inner city wall, past the guards at the gate, past the tall tenements where the buildings lean and whisper to each other, where the residents fly their underpants like flags. Further on, to the last of the city.

Here, long ago bombs have brought underground rivers to the surface and made a misery factory of the suburbs. Here we find Rupi's family home. A house hunched for comfort in the arms of a dead willow.

Crouch with me on the floor, where toadstools prise loose the skirting boards. Rupi's mother mashes bog garlic in a pestle. The smell is so strong that the dragonflies swoon.

The crumpled house is now quiet. Tuli, her youngest child and only girl, has finally fallen asleep, her cheeks red with teething. If Rupi's family had the means, there would be painkillers for Tuli. Her only relief would not be chewing on a flannel cooled in a cup of water.

Rupi's dad comes back from the stream with a bucket full of crayfish. Only here, on this revolting circumference of the city, are tastebuds dull enough to eat these armoured shit-scoffers.

Rupi usually likes to kill the crayfish, but he and his brothers are late again.

Let's go to Rupi's brothers now.

They've been patient for so long, hidden behind the mouth of the underpass. The ferns are cool against their backs. Their soiled clothes blend so well against the wall. They are almost as invisible as we are.

Now, this is what they've waited for.

This is the moment I wanted you to see. I hope that you too have a taste for the unusual. For the brutal.

If you look now, out of the corner of your eye, maybe you'll see the rest of us, sitting on the canal edge, perched upon the roofs, laid out along the top of the walls. We are all so light we could not break the thinnest neck of the thinnest fungus. Our most violent action would struggle to loose a single petal. But we are not here to act. We are here to watch.

And listen.

Here come the pounding footfalls of a boy on the run.

Behind the mouth of the underpass, Rupi's brothers clutch nets in their claws.

At the same moment, in the market square, Alice's heel breaks and she falls. Her bony bottom hits the cobbles hard.

In the crumpled house of Rupi's parents, Rupi's dad hits the hilt of a kitchen knife with the heel of his hand and drives the blade tip through the crayfish's helmet.

And behind the window too green to see through, Danya tells Morris to hang on. Just the flash of a canine in the snarl of her mouth is enough to delay his orgasm. Her eyes squeeze tight with concentration. Her heels push into the mattress. Her head tilts back and her wet throat arches. Morris bears this delicious agony for a moment, then tells her he can't hold on any longer, and pulls out. Neither of them wants to risk conceiving a child in this city. His erection twangs a chord in the soupy air, and he grabs a t-shirt from the bed to suffocate it. His knees hit the floorboards as his spores fly.

Here is Rupi, in the underpass. Mouth open, lungs empty, eyes wide, pushing through the last moments of this chase. His brothers do not pat him on the back as he passes, but their thoughts are saturated with pride.

The pursuers come. Ragged. Angry. Mindless. The fish forgotten. They imagine braining the youth with their sticks. This is what keeps them going. But before we see the moment we have been waiting for, I want you to notice something.

Look how the men have changed.

They are not nearly so fearsome now. Now that we stand behind Rupi's brothers. Maybe we even feel a little sorry for them. Maybe we don't.

The police are in the underpass, and at the moment that their bootfalls bounce off the walls, Rupi's brothers raise the net and the three pursuers spill into it, become tangled, their fingers and feet caught up within its holes. They are knotted as they hit the cobbles, and even while they fall, the brothers work fast applying a second net, wrapping it around.

Rupi drops to the ground, heaving in every breath. He is shaking. His blood is hot in his face. Maybe like this, he senses us for a second, all of us, but not fully. To him, we are aberrations of light, symptoms of exhaustion.

The policemen howl curses. Threaten terrible punishments. Rupi's brothers stuff big kicks into the nets, then drag the policemen to the edge of the canal and jump in with them, pulling them under.

We will wait above the water, because this is where it is best.

The heads of Rupi's brothers break the surface. They spit green water from their mouths and shake their wet hair away from their eyes. The only thing to reveal the violent panic beneath the surface is the tremor of their shoulders.

These moments are still and long compared to the frenzy of the chase. How precious does each of our breaths feel now? Rupi's hands are trembling on his knees. The brothers look to each other, wondering whether the job is done yet.

In the market, Braughin helps Alice to her feet. She is sweating and humiliated because everyone has stopped to watch her. This is an ill omen for her evening. She remembers her sister's fall down to John Hopworth's and is afraid.

Behind the greened-out window, Morris throws his impregnated t-shirt into the wash basket while Danya stands at the sink. She fills her cupped hands with cold water, and with it shocks her face.

At Rupi's house, the crayfish gasp in the pan. And at the canal, crayfish cling to the nets with their pincers as Rupi helps his brothers haul the men out. The boys drip water and weed all over the canal-side.

They stop at the sound of rubber brakes squeezing a bicycle wheel still.

The old man who has seen them and frozen, stares for only a second, before swinging his bike back the way he came. The boys watch him retreat, water streaming from their chins, until the rattle of his pedals is gone.

There is not much more to see now, and already the other observers are moving away, sniffing out more drama. And this city is rank with it. It gurgles in every drain.

We will stay for just a moment. Watch the boys prise the dead fingers from the nets. Sit the bodies up against the wall. Wrap the policemen's arms around each other's shoulders. Laugh at the affectionate way two of the three heads have lolled together.

Inside Rupi's jacket, the mouth of the stolen fish is agape.

Let's leave now, before the boys roll up their nets, sling them over their shoulders and head for home. We should not be alone with the men on the canalside.

Tamagotchi

My son's Tamagotchi had AIDS. The virtual pet was rendered on the little LCD screen with no more than 30 pixels, but the sickness was obvious. It had that AIDS look, you know? It was thinner than it had been. Some of its pixels were faded, and the pupils of its huge eyes were smaller, giving it an empty stare.

I had bought the Tamagotchi, named Meemoo, for Luke just a couple of weeks ago. He had really wanted a kitten, but Gabby did not want a cat in the house. 'A cat will bring in dead birds and toxoplasmosis,' she said, her fingers spread protectively over her bulging stomach.

A Tamagotchi had seemed like the perfect compromise – something for Luke to empathise with and to look after, to teach him the rudiments of petcare for a time after the baby had been born. Empathy is one of the things that the book said Luke would struggle with. He would have difficulty reading facial expressions. The Tamagotchi had only three different faces, so it would be good practice for him.

Together, Luke and I watched Meemoo curled in the corner of its screen. Sometimes, Meemoo would get up, limp to the opposite corner, and produce a pile of something. I don't know what this something was, or which orifice it came from – the resolution was not good enough to tell.

'You're feeding it too much,' I told Luke. He said that he wasn't, but he'd been sitting on the sofa thumbing the buttons for hours at a time, so I'm sure he must have been.

There's not much else to do with a Tamagotchi.

I read the instruction manual that came with Meemoo. Its needs were simple: food, water, sleep, play. Meemoo was supposed to give signals when it required one of these things. Luke's job as Meemoo's carer was to press the appropriate button at the appropriate time. The manual said that overfeeding, underfeeding, lack of exercise and unhappiness could all make a Tamagotchi sick. A little black skull and crossbones should appear on the screen when this happens, and by pressing button A twice, then B, one could administer medicine. The instructions said that sometimes it might take two or three shots of medicine, depending on how sick your Tamagotchi is.

I checked Meemoo's screen again and there was no skull and crossbones.

The instructions said that if the Tamagotchi dies, you have to stick a pencil into the hole in its back to reset it. A new creature would then be born.

When Luke had finally gone to sleep and could not see me molesting his virtual pet, I found the hole in Meemoo's back and jabbed a sharpened pencil into it. But when I turned it back over, Meemoo was still there, as sick as ever. I jabbed a few more times and tried it with a pin too, in case I wasn't getting in deep enough. But it wouldn't reset.

I wondered what happened if Meemoo died, now that its reset button didn't work. Was there a malfunction that had robbed Luke's Tamagotchi of its immortality? Did it have just one shot at life? I guess that made it a lot more special, and in a small way, it made me more determined to find a cure for Meemoo.

I plugged Meemoo into my PC – a new feature in this generation of Tamagotchis. I hoped that some kind of diagnostics wizard would pop up and sort it out.

A Tamagotchi screen blinked into life on my PC. There were many big-eyed mutant creatures jiggling for attention, including another Meemoo, looking like its picture on the box, before it got sick. One of the options on the screen was 'sync your Tamagotchi'.

When I did this, Meemoo's limited world of square grey pixels was transformed into a full colour three-dimensional animation on my screen. The blank room in which it lived was revealed as a conservatory filled with impossible plants growing under the pale-pink Tamagotchi sun. And in the middle of this world, lying on the carpet, was Meemoo.

It looked awful. In this fully realised version of the Tamagotchi's room, Meemoo was a shrivelled thing. The skin on its feet was dry and peeling. Its eyes, once bright white with crisp highlights, were yellow and unreflective. There were scabs around the base of its nose. I wondered what kind of demented mind would create a child's toy that was capable of reaching such abject deterioration.

I clicked through every button available until I found the medical kit. From this you could drag and drop pills onto the Tamagotchi. I guess Meemoo was supposed to eat or absorb these, but they just hovered in front of it, as if Meemoo was refusing to take its medicine.

I tried the same trick with Meemoo that I do with Luke to get him to take his medicine. I mixed it with food. I dragged a chicken drumstick from the food store and put it on top of the medicine, hoping that Meemoo would get up and eat them both. But it just lay there, looking at me, its mouth slightly open. Its look of sickness was so convincing that I could practically smell its foul breath coming from the screen.

I sent Meemoo's makers a sarcastic e-mail describing its condition and asking what needed to be done to restore its health.

A week later, I had received no reply and Meemoo was getting even worse. There were pale grey dots appearing on it. When I synced Meemoo to my computer, these dots were revealed as deep red sores. And the way the light from the Tamagotchi sun reflected off them, you could tell they were wet.

I went to a toyshop and showed them the Tamagotchi. 'I've not seen one do that before,' the girl behind the counter said. 'Must be something the new ones do.'

I came home from work one day to find Luke had a friend over for a play-date. The friend was called Becky, and she had a Tamagotchi too. Gabby was trying to organise at least one play-date a week to help Luke socialise.

Becky's Tamagotchi gave me an idea.

This generation of Tamagotchis had the ability to connect to other Tamagotchis. By getting your Tamagotchi within a metre of a friend's, your virtual pets could play games or dance together. Maybe if I connected the two Tamagotchis, the medicine button in Becky's would cure Meemoo.

At first, Luke violently resisted giving Meemoo to me, despite me saying I only wanted to help it. But when I bribed Luke and Becky with chocolate biscuits and a packet of crisps, they agreed to hand them over.

When Gabby came in from hanging up the washing, she was furious.

'Why'd you give the kids crisps and chocolate?' she said, slamming the empty basket on the ground. 'I'm just about to give them dinner.'

'Leave me alone for a sec,' I said. I didn't have time to explain. I had only a few minutes before the kids would demand their toys back, and I was having trouble getting the Tamagotchis to find each other – maybe Meemoo's Bluetooth connection had been compromised by the virus.

Eventually though, when I put their connectors right next to each other, they made a synchronous pinging sound, and both characters appeared on both screens. It's amazing how satisfying that was.

Meemoo looked sick on Becky's screen too. I pressed A twice and then B to administer medicine.

Nothing happened.

I tried again. But the Tamagotchis just stood there. One healthy, one sick. Doing nothing.

Luke and Becky came back, their fingers oily and their faces brown with chocolate. I told them to wipe their hands on their trousers before they played with their Tamagotchis. I was about to disconnect them from each other, but when they saw that they had each other's characters on their screens, they got excited and sat at the kitchen table to play together.

I poured myself a beer, and for Gabby a half glass of wine (her daily limit), then, seeing the crisps out on the side, I helped myself to a bag.

Later, when my beer was finished and it was time for Becky's mum to pick her up, Becky handed me her Tamagotchi.

'Can you fix Weebee?' she asked.

Becky's pink Tamagotchi was already presenting the first symptoms of Meemoo's disease: the thinning and greying of features, the stoop, the lethargy.

I heard Becky's mum pull up in the car as I began to press the medicine buttons, knowing already that they would not work. 'It just needs some rest,' I said. 'Leave it alone until tomorrow, and it should be okay.'

Luke had been invited to a birthday party. Usually Gabby would take Luke to parties, but she was feeling rough – she was having a particularly unpleasant first trimester this time. So she persuaded me to go, even though I hate kids' parties.

I noticed that lots of other kids at the party had Tamagotchis fastened to the belt loops of their skirts and trousers. The kids would stop every few minutes during their games to lift up their Tamagotchis and check they were okay, occasionally pressing a button to satisfy one of their needs.

'These Tamagotchis are insane, aren't they?' I remarked to another dad who was standing at the edge of the garden with his arms folded across his chest.

'Yeah,' he smiled.

'My kid's one got sick,' I said. 'One of its arms fell off this morning. Can you believe that?'

The dad turned to me, his face suddenly serious. 'You're not Luke's dad, are you?' he asked.

'I am,' I said.

'I had to buy a new Tamagotchi thanks to you.'

I frowned and smirked, thinking that he couldn't be serious, but my expression seemed to piss him off.

'You had Becky Willis over at your house, didn't you?' he continued. 'Her pet got Matty's pet sick 'cause she sits next to him in class. My boy's pet died. I've half a mind to charge you for the new one.'

I stared right into his eyes, looking for an indication that he was joking, but there was none. 'I don't know what to say,' I said. And truly, I didn't. I thought he was crazy, especially the way he referred to the Tamagotchis as 'pets', like they were real pets, not just 30 pixels on an LCD screen with only a little more functionality than my alarm clock. 'Maybe there was something else wrong with yours. Luke's didn't die.'

The other dad shook his head and blew out, and then turned sideways to look at me, making a crease in his fat neck. 'You didn't bring it here, did you?' he said.

'Well, Luke takes it everywhere with him,' I said.

'Jesus,' he said, and then he literally ran across a game of Twister that some of the kids were playing to grab his son's Tamagotchi and check that it was okay. He had an argument with his son as he detached it from the boy's belt loop, saying he was going to put it in the car for safety. They were making so much noise that the mother of the kid having the birthday came over to calm them. The dad leaned in close to her to whisper, and she looked at the ground while he spoke, then up at me, then at Luke.

She headed across the garden towards me.

'Hi there. We've not met before,' she said, offering her hand with a pretty smile. 'I'm Lillian, Jake's mum.' We shook hands and I said that it was nice to meet her. 'We're just about to play pass the parcel,' she said.

'Oh right.'

'Yes, and I'm concerned about the other children catching...' She opened her mouth, showing that her teeth were clenched together, and she nodded, hoping that I understood, that she wouldn't need to suffer the embarrassment of spelling it out.

'It's just a toy,' I said.

'Still, I'd prefer...'

'You make it sound like...'

'If you wouldn't mind...'

I shook my head at the lunacy of the situation, but agreed to take care of it.

When I told Luke I had to take Meemoo away for a minute he went apeshit. He stamped and he made his hand into the shape of a claw and yelled, 'Sky badger!'

When Luke does sky badger, anyone in a two-metre radius gets hurt. Sky badger is vicious. His sharp fingernails rake forearms. He goes for the eyes.

'Okay okay,' I said, backing away and putting my hands up defensively. 'You can keep hold of Meemoo, but I'll have to take you home then.'

Luke screwed up his nose and frowned so deeply that I could barely see his dark eyes.

'You'll miss out on the birthday cake,' I added.

Luke relaxed his talons and handed Meemoo to me, making a growl as he did so. Meemoo was hot, and I wondered whether it was from Luke's sweaty hands or if the Tamagotchi had a fever.

I held Luke's hand and took him over to where the pass-the-parcel ring was being straightened out by some of the mums, stashing Meemoo out of sight in my pocket. I sat Luke down and explained to him what would happen and what he was expected to do. A skinny kid with two front teeth missing looked at me and Luke, wondering what our deal was.

I had to wait until Monday to check my e-mails at work. There was still nothing from the makers of Tamagotchi. At lunch, while I splashed Bolognese sauce over my keyboard, I Googled 'Tamagotchi' along with every synonym for 'virus'. I could find nothing other than the standard instructions to give it medicine when the skull and crossbones appeared.

Half way through the afternoon, while I was in my penultimate meeting of the day, a tannoy announcement asked me to call reception. When a tannoy goes out, everyone knows it's an emergency, and when it's for me, everyone knows it's something to do with Luke. I stepped out of the meeting room and ran back to my desk, trying hard not to look at all the heads turning towards me.

Gabby was on hold. When reception put her through, she was crying. Luke had had one of his fits. A short one this time, for him, just eight minutes, but since he'd come round, the right side of his body was paralysed. This was something new. It terrified me that his fits were changing, that they might be developing in some way. I told Gabby to stay calm and that I would leave right away.

When I got home, the ambulance was still parked outside, but the crew were packing away their kit. 'He's okay,' one of the ambulance men said as I ran up the drive.

Luke's paralysis had lasted 15 minutes after the seizure had finished, but now he was moving normally again, except for a limpness at the edge of his mouth that made him slur his words. The ambulance man said this happens sometimes, so we needn't worry.

I hugged Luke, burying my lips into his thick hair and kissing the side of his head, wishing that we lived in a world where kisses could fix brains. I stroked his back, hoping that maybe I would find a little reset button there, sunk into a hole, something I could prod that would let us start over, that would wipe all the scribbles from the slate and leave it blank again.

Gabby was sitting on the edge of the armchair holding her stomach.

'Are you okay?' I asked.

She nodded, taking a tissue from the sleeve of her cardigan and wiping her nose. Gabby's biggest fear was that Luke's problems weren't just a part of him, but part of the factory that had made him – what if every kid we produced together had the same design fault?

The doctors had all said that the chances of it happening twice were tiny, but I don't think we'd ever be able to fully relax. I knew that long after our second kid was born, we'd both be looking out for the diagnostic signs that had seemed so innocuous at first with Luke.

A letter came home from school banning Tamagotchis. Another three kids' Tamagotchis had died and could not be resurrected.

'People are blanking me when I drop Luke off in the morning,' Gabby said. She was rubbing her fingers into her temples.

The situation had gone too far. Meemoo would have to go.

When I went to tell Luke that he'd have to say goodbye to Meemoo, he was sitting on the edge of the sand pit injecting the sand with a yellow straw.

'No!' he barked at me, and made that frown-face of his. He gripped Meemoo in his fist and folded his arms across his chest.

Gabby came outside with her book. 'Help me out will you?' I asked.

'You can handle this for a change,' she said.

I tried bribing Luke with a biscuit, but he just got angrier. I tried lying to him, saying that I needed to take Meemoo to hospital to make him better, but I had lost his trust. Eventually, I had only one option left. I told Luke that he had to tidy up his toys in the garden or I'd have to confiscate Meemoo for two whole days. I knew that Luke would never clean up his toys. The bit of his brain in charge of tidying up must have been within the damaged area. But I went through the drama of asking him a few times, and, as he got more irate, stamping and kicking things, I began to count.

'Don't count!' he said, knowing the finality of a countdown.

'Come on,' I said. 'You've got four seconds left. Just pick up your toys and you can keep Meemoo.'

If he'd actually picked up his toys then, it would have been such a miracle that I would have let him keep Meemoo, AIDS and all.

'Three...two...'

'Stop counting!' Luke screamed, and then the dreaded, 'Sky badger!'

Luke's fingers curled into that familiar and frightening shape and he came after me. I skipped away from him, tripping over a bucket.

'One and a half....one...come on, you've only got half a second left.' A part of me must have been enjoying this, because I was giggling.

'Stop it,' Gabby said. 'You're being cruel.'

'He's got to learn,' I said. 'Come on Luke, you've only got a fraction of a second left. Start picking up your toys now and you can keep Meemoo.'

Luke roared and swung sky badger at me, at my arms, at my face. I grabbed him round the waist and turned him so that his back was towards me. Sky badger sunk his claws into my knuckles while I wrestled Meemoo out of his other hand.

By the time I'd got Meemoo away, there were three crescent-shaped gouges out of my knuckles, and they were stinging like crazy.

'I HATE YOU!' Luke screamed, crying. He stormed inside and slammed the door behind him.

'You deserved that,' Gabby said, looking over the top of her sunglasses.

I couldn't just throw Meemoo away. Luke would never forgive me for that. It might become one of those formative moments, something that would forever warp him and give him all kinds of trust issues in later life. Instead, I planned to euthanize Meemoo.

If I locked Meemoo in the medicine cabinet, taking away the things that were helping it survive: food, play, petting and the toilet, the AIDS would get stronger as it got weaker and surrounded by more of its effluence. The AIDS would win. And when Meemoo was dead, it would either reset itself as a healthy Tamagotchi, or it would die. If it was healthy, Luke could have it back; if it died, then Luke would learn a valuable lesson about mortality and I would buy him a new one to cheer him up.

It was tempting while Meemoo was in the cabinet to sneak a peek, to watch for its final moments, but the Tamagotchi had sensors that picked up movement. It might interpret my attention as caring, and gain some extra power to resist the virus destroying it. No, I had to leave it alone, despite the temptation.

Meemoo's presence inside the medicine cabinet seemed to transform the cabinet's outward appearance. It went from being an ordinary medicine cabinet to being something else, something... other.

After two whole days, I could resist no longer. I was certain that Meemoo must have perished by now. Luke was insistent about being there when I opened up the cabinet, and I did not have the strength for an argument.

'Okay,' I said. 'But have you learned your lesson about tidying up?'

'Give it back,' he said, pouting.

I opened the cupboard and took out the Tamagotchi.

Meemo was alive.

It had now lost three of its limbs, having just one arm left, which was stretched out under its head. One of its eyes had closed up to a small unseeing dot. Its pixellated circumference was broken in places, wide open pores through which invisible things must surely be entering and escaping.

'This is ridiculous,' I said. 'Luke, I'm sorry, but we're going to have to throw him away.'

Luke snatched the Tamagotchi from me and ran to Gabby, screaming. He was shaking, his face red and sweaty.

'What have you done now?' Gabby scowled at me.

I held my forehead with both hands. 'I give up,' I said, and stomped upstairs to the bedroom.

I put on the TV and watched a cookery show. There was something soothing in the way the chef was searing the tuna in the pan that let my heartbeats soften by degrees.

Gabby called me from downstairs. 'Can you come and get Luke in? Dinner's almost ready.'

I let my feet slip over the edge of each step, enjoying the pressure against the soles of my feet. I went outside in my socks. Luke was burying a football in the sandpit.

'Time to come in little man,' I said. 'Dinner's ready.'

He ignored me.

'Come in Luke,' Gabby called through the open window, and at the sound of his mum's voice, Luke got up, brushed the sand from his jeans, and went inside, giving me a wide berth as he ran past.

A drop of rain hit the tip of my nose. The clouds above were low and heavy. The ragged kind that can take days to drain. As I turned to go inside, I noticed that Luke had left Meemoo on the edge of the sandpit. I started to reach down for it, but then stopped, stood up, and went inside, closing the door behind me.

After dinner, it was Gabby's turn to take Luke to bed. I made tea and leaned over the back of the sofa, resting my cup and my elbows on the windowsill and inhaling the hot steam. Outside, the rain was pounding the grass, making craters in the sandpit, and bouncing off of the Tamagotchi. I thought how ridiculous it was that I was feeling guilty, but out of some strange duty I continued to watch it, until the rain had washed all the light out of the sky.

Without a Shell

THE TASTE OF porridge was still in Bucky's mouth when he saw the guy explode. First, there was a flash, like fireworks on the ground, then the crack and boom of the soundwave rolling out across the pavement, flipping cars up onto their backs, throwing kids against the school railings. For the briefest moment, Bucky saw the guy come apart, his insides effervescing, continuing in the direction he had been running before he detonated himself. And then the explosion picked Bucky up, rattling against his visor, and dumped him into a privet hedge.

There were shouts, and the roar of fire exhausting itself on the inside of a pizza van. Teachers calling everyone inside. The sounds that always came before the sirens.

In assembly, they all lay on their backs on the hall floor with their eyes closed. The place stank of smoke and static and shoe leather. An old CD of nineties pop hits played through the PA system. The voice of the singer repeating the invitation 'come on Barbie, let's go party' almost smothered the sounds of their uniforms working.

All around Bucky, the uniforms purred against the battered bodies of the students, teasing out their bruises, anaesthetising their cuts, sewing back together their skin. Bucky's collar worked at his neck, licking out the stickiness where a branch had torn into him.

The teachers sat on chairs at the side of the hall. A chunk of Mrs Abernethy's frizzy white hair was missing at the side, the ends blackened where it had been. Her eyes were closed and her little fists were on her lap.

When all the uniforms were silent, the sound of the music was faded out slowly, easing everyone back into themselves. They sat up, cross-legged, as Mrs Abernethy climbed the stairs to the stage and took her position behind the lectern. Here, backlit by the screen, the bite taken from her bonnet was obvious to all, and a murmur spread among them.

'Yes,' Mrs Abernethy began. 'A warning to me, to us all, to never be without our full guard.' The murmuring grew louder, but she stopped it just by straightening her neck.

Next to Bucky, Dill whispered, 'Shame it didn't take her bloody head off.'

Bucky lifted the fingers of one hand, a signal that silenced Dill.

'Once when I was a girl,' Mrs Abernethy continued, 'I was putting on a pair of dungarees, which I'd just taken from the airing cupboard, when I felt a strange buzzing sensation, and then a sharp sting in my side. A honey bee had flown inside them while they hung on the line, and then my mother had unknowingly folded the bee inside the clothes, where it had stayed silent all night until I disturbed it. It was the first time I'd ever been stung, and the shock made the pain much worse than it really was. I made a terrible fuss and brought my mother running upstairs. She thought something truly awful had happened to me. Once I was out of my dungarees, my mother shook them, and the bee fell out and crawled across my bedroom carpet. My side was throbbing. It was the most ugly pain I'd ever felt. I was so angry with this bee that I picked up a book to dash its little brains on my floor. But before I got to it, the bee flew up and out of the window. My mother told me not to worry, that it was already dead, because a honey bee's sting, once thrust into skin, is ripped from the bee's body, along with some of its insides. It would soon be dead, and no longer had the means to harm anyone else.' Mrs Abernethy paused and looked at the students, her fingers coming to the edge of the lectern for emphasis. 'At least the bastards always die,' she said. 'At least we have that.'

The first time Bucky had put the uniform on, his mum cried as she smoothed the fabric over his arms and squeezed his shoulders. He asked her what was wrong, but she shook her head. He never understood what was going on with her. Was she proud of him because of everything the uniform signified, or was she afraid for him, knowing that the uniform would make him stand out, would incite jealousy and rage?

Before Bucky's school had the uniforms, the attacks were few and randomly spread among all of the city's schools. But giving these children special protection made them a special target. The suicide bombers knew exactly whom this country least wanted to lose. The uniforms also made the job easier for the conscientious bomber, because they could complete their mission knowing that it would achieve its objective of increasing terror and newspaper columns without doing any permanent damage to the kids.

It was like they said: if there was a nuclear strike, the only things left standing would be the roaches and the kids of Aleksander Academy.

Gym class. They played football in their house teams for points. Bucky was in Radcliffe, the blue house. At the other end of the gym, the five Skinner kids in green were on the balls of their feet, ready to move.

The whistle blew, and Mr Castle chucked the ball into the centre. Bucky ran for it. Gayle, his mirror position on the other side, ran too. Her white mouth guard filled the whole of her snarl. Her ponytail lashed her back. He could not look at Gayle without feeling the familiar cold slam of his back hitting the gymnasium floor. But today, he was determined to stay on his feet.

His heart was thumping, his breath loud in his mouth.

At the last second, as she was almost upon him, he dodged to her left side, stretching out his arm to whack her in the chest and knock her to the ground. But just before running into the bar of his forearm, she swivelled, the sole of her plimsolls squeaking. In two great bounds she leapt up onto his thigh, then his shoulder, and stamped on the back of the head as she sailed over him.

Bucky's hand hit the floor first, then his face. He heard the thwack and smack of Gayle kicking the ball and the ball striking the wall on which the goal was painted. The whistle blew. Bucky's glove tightened with brutal force, cracking and fizzing as it set his broken metacarpal.

'Ten points Skinner!' Mr Castle announced, and then blew his whistle again. 'Someone get him off the court.'

'You suck,' Gayle said, grabbing Bucky by the foot and pulling him to the side. Bucky tried to get up, but the room was swirling. He lay there, focusing on a Kit-Kat wrapper under the bench, willing everything to stop so he could get up and re-join the game.

Gayle Hopper. Whose symmetry was flawless, whose socks were always pulled up, who had once killed a kid.

That's what she'd told him anyway, the first time they went out on a date. And it wasn't really a date. He had not asked her, and she had not accepted. They just walked home together after school, taking the long route, and sat on the old railway bridge throwing stones at the abandoned greenhouses below.

They sucked fizzy lemon sweets, smacking their lips while they talked. She asked him if it was true about his dad getting his head cut off, and he said that it was, knowing that she had already watched the whole thing on YouTube. Everyone at school had. But that she had asked meant she wanted him to think she hadn't watched it, which meant she wanted him to like her. And that made him excited.

'How do you even cope with something like that?' she asked.

'You just do,' he shrugged.

She'd rested her chin on her folded arms on the railings and looked out across the rooftops.

'So is it true that you killed someone?' he asked.

'I don't like to talk about it,' she said, loftily. But after a moment of noisy sweet-sucking, she relented.

Just after they had all been issued their nano-tech military-grade uniforms, there were almost daily clashes between Aleksander Academy and the local comprehensive, known as St Fuckwits.

A schoolbus had been blown up at St Fuckwits a few months before, but they were offered no special protection. Battles were played out on the local news between parents and school governors, and on the playing fields behind Sainsbury's by the pupils themselves.

At these battles, there were always more kids from St Fuckwits than from Aleksanders – Fuckwits had 800 pupils, compared to Aleksanders' 60, but their aim was rubbish and they had regular uniforms.

Bucky had not been at this particular clash, but Gayle said that one of the Fuckwits kids had tossed a hub-cap like a Frisbee, and it had smacked her in the visor and made her stumble. Gayle never stumbles. She was mad. She picked the hub-cap straight back up again and grunted as she threw it at the kid. Gayle's aim was perfect. She got the kid straight in the throat and he went down like a sack of shit.

Bucky didn't ask Gayle how come she didn't get arrested if she'd killed a kid. It would have popped the bubble they were blowing together.

The first scrap Bucky ever went to, when he got a freckled kid right in the forehead with a pebble and he went down, Gayle had patted his arm and said, 'good one,' and then told him not to worry, that these kids didn't cost their parents anything to make. If any of them didn't get up again, their mum and dad could make another one for free.

After Bucky had walked Gayle to her house, he got home two hours late to find his mum standing in the open doorway, the smell of chicken soup pouring out into the street. He tried to explain that his phone had ran out of charge, that he'd had his first date with a girl, something which he was certain she'd be proud of. But she didn't hear. Her ears were stuffed full of madness.

Whenever Bucky's mum had to punish him, she did it with the bamboo handle of a broken fly-swat. The swatting bit broke off years ago, but she kept the handle tucked down the side of the fridge. When it needed taking out, she would brush off the dust with her fingers first, a habit which always puzzled Bucky, as his trousers would clean off the dust anyway. It bothered him that this made no sense. Maybe if he understood it, he would understand a lot of other stuff too. Things were rarely explained to Bucky, and he suspected that this was because people were afraid of finding out they were less smart than he was.

His mum's cheeks were always red after she'd given him a beating. He didn't know whether this was because it pained her to have to punish him, or if it was a biological reaction to the effort needed to damage him through the uniform.

After a beating, the walk upstairs was always a slow one, and his mum watched him climb, one step at a time. 'Make sure you sit on it for half an hour,' she would say. This was to make sure the suit had time to repair everything, for the little nanotubes to identify the damage and begin their healing regime. If Bucky took off his uniform before the damage was healed, the evidence would remain on him until the next morning when he went to school.

When he sat on his bed, he could feel the seat of his trousers weaving everything back into place, an itchy, buzzing sensation, like he was sitting on a nest of angry ants. From here, he had a clear view right across the common to the school clocktower with its broken face. At dusk, its silhouette was a forlorn shape, hunkered down atop the gymnasium, its head tucked into its shoulders.

In the queue for lunch, Bucky was standing next to Dill. There was a desperation in Dill's eagerness which most people found repellent, but Bucky was too polite to ignore him. Something about Dill's enthusiasm always drew him in eventually. Dill kicked Bucky's shoe and grinned. 'Where did you tell your mum you're going tonight?' he asked.

'Extra football practice,' Bucky said. He took a bowl of green jelly from the fridge and put it on his tray. He'd split his lip when he hit the gym floor, and couldn't face eating the spaghetti Bolognese, which he knew would make the cut sting like crazy. His reflection wobbled on the jelly's surface.

'I told mine I was coming to your house,' Dill said.

Bucky chewed the inside of his cheek, wondering whether Dill's parents had his home phone number, and whether they might call for any reason. He pictured his mum picking up the phone, and her jaw going tight as his lie was revealed.

He and Dill sat with the other Radcliffes. At the table opposite, Gayle made the face that they made when they were pretending to be Fuckwits, stabbing her knife up and down.

Dill laughed beside him, spitting Bolognese onto the table. 'Better hope you don't get her tonight.'

The speed at which Gayle's affection for Bucky had soured astounded him. For a month after they had walked home together, she sought him out at breaktimes so their phones could mate, swapping their favourite music and photos of themselves. They sipped from the same paper cups. One time she'd even feigned stupidity for him, the most selfless gift in an Aleksanders' courtship. She pretended she could not identify the third nominalisation in a given sentence during the inter-house quiz, allowing Bucky to win that round.

Inter-house competition was encouraged with spit-flying fervour at Aleksanders. The captain of Radcliffe, Valdez, was insane with it, whipping them up into a frenzy of excitement with his legendary pre-competition rhetoric, then giving dreadful beastings in the bogs to anyone who messed up.

Valdez was huge, so Bucky really had no choice but to tackle Gayle at that football match. He'd tried to ease her down as gently as possible. He hadn't meant to knock her out. His head just got in the way.

She'd remained unconscious at the side of the field while Radcliffe roared with celebration, piling into each other. Bucky, dripping with mud, experienced true regret for the first time, and nothing in his uniform was able to heal it.

In study period, Bucky was reading Weschler's *History of the Use of Metaphor in Warfare* when Gayle elbowed him in the back of the head.

'Fuckwit,' she said, and her fellow Skinners tittered behind her.

Bucky imagined the troops in Iran, and the terrifying hardship they were enduring. In the mountains, they were being attacked with projectiles made of intelligent stuff that burned long after impact, that was designed to sniff out flesh and eat through nano-fabrics to find it. These soldiers did not lie down to allow their uniforms to heal their bodies; they continued to fight while their uniforms worked. It made the attacks that Aleksanders' pupils suffered at the hands of KKD supporters seem trivial.

Our soldiers had minds trained to resist sleep, to act without hesitation, to attack with relentless spirit. The officers who were Aleksanders graduates had a reputation for stretching the capabilities of the ordinary soldier until they began to act like specials themselves.

Mr Wotek, Bucky's Neuro-Linguistics teacher, said that

by the time Bucky was ready to graduate, there would be positions for specialist Neuros who would never step onto the battle ground, but would work in labs creating Think-Weapons – something that was science-fiction now but on the cusp of reality. Mr Wotek said Bucky had a natural flair for Neuro. He didn't know if it was natural or not, but it was definitely what he wanted to do.

If Bucky's dad had been better trained, if he'd been wearing the second generation of nano-uniforms and not the first, he would not have been captured. He would not have appeared on YouTube surrounded by KKD soldiers, one of them shaking a sack at the camera. The same sack that minutes later would contain his head.

In the last class of the day, Bucky listened to the other kids' feet jiggling under their chairs. They couldn't wait for the bell to go. In his head, these little foot tappings, which the teacher's ears were too weak to pick up, were like drumbeats.

The school bell rang. They stuffed their notebooks into their bags and slid their chairs under their desks. There was excited chatter, which no teacher bothered to stifle. Bucky saw Gayle give another Skinner a covert thumbs-up. Their shared anticipation made Bucky shiver.

The Rec-Centre playground was filled with the clicks of spinning bicycle wheels. The youngest person present, Taylor, an eight-year-old girl from Mattock, set each of the empty wine bottles in a line as fellow Mattocks fished them out of the recycling bin and handed them to her.

One person from each of the four houses was selected with *ipp-dip-dog-shit*. Those four then stepped forward and faced each other in a circle. Little Taylor put an empty red wine bottle on the ground in the centre of the circle and spun it. It stopped first at Dill from Pearson and then at Huck Yama from Mattock. There were gasps and chuckles because

Yama was a monstrous fifteen-year-old built like a bison and had never been knocked off his bike, whereas Dill was thirteen and had yet to win a round.

Bucky patted Dill on the back. 'He's terrified of losing to you,' Bucky said.

Yama and Dill each took a bottle from the line and smashed off the bottom against the side of the recycling bin. They took bikes from their housemates and cycled up to either end of the alleyway that ran along the length of the playground, where they faced each other, waiting. The alleyway was narrow, on one side a red brick wall, on the other, the wire link playground fence.

The kids from Aleksanders clung to the playground side of the fence, shaking it and shouting the names of the opponents.

Little Taylor looked across to both ends of the alley to make sure they were ready, then called out, 'Ichi, ni, san!'

Yama was fastest from the start. Reflections of the buddleia that overhung the alley whizzed across his visor. Panic made Dill's feet keep missing the pedals.

Speed was the key to bottle jousting. The playground entrance was directly central between the two start points, so if they travelled at the same speed, the clash would happen there. If one of the combatants could cover more ground though, they would force the moment of clashing inside their opponent's half of the alley. If you managed to do this, you had a huge psychological advantage.

Yama and Dill met half way up Dill's run. Yama lanced him in the chest with the broken bottle so hard that it shoved him off the back of his bike. Dill's back hit the ground first, his unused bottle smashing beside him. Yama continued on, cycling over Dill's arm, and chucking the bottle down so it cracked on his helmet. He thrust his fist up into the air to wild cries of excitement from his housemates. Dill's bike, as if only just realising its rider was gone, fell sideways and scraped against the brick wall.

Three Pearsons ran up the alley to grab their unconscious housemate and lifted him inside the playground. They put him on the roundabout, where he lay, his uniform fizzing against his bruised chest.

The kids had to move fast now. They usually only got in two or three rounds before the police sirens sounded and they had to run. Bucky was picked in the next four, as was Gayle. When little Taylor span the bottle, it stopped at Gayle. When it span a second time, Gayle stepped on it so that it stopped in front of Bucky. To argue would have been cowardly.

Gayle picked up two bottles and clashed them together to break the bottoms off. She threw one of them to him and he jumped aside rather than attempting to catch it. It shattered around his feet and the Skinners laughed, and called him chicken-shit. Bucky picked up a bottle, whacked it against the container, and wondered how one simple mistake on his part could have turned Gayle into this mad bull who couldn't wait to gore him. Was it always going to be like this with her? Did he have another four years of it before he graduated?

Bucky cycled up to his end of the alley, the left hand end, looking at all the kids' fingers poking through the fence.

He turned and faced Gayle. She was leaning over her handlebars, nodding and glaring in his direction. Little Taylor took her position and held her arm in the air.

Bucky stuck his hand up to stop little Taylor. He put his bottle down on the ground beside him, then began to undo the buttons of his jacket. He ignored the confused murmurs from behind the fence, and stared straight at Gayle as he pulled his arms out of the sleeves, folded the jacket, and put it on the ground. Gayle did not move until he started on his shirt buttons. She stood up on the pedals of her bike, leaning against the wall, perplexity showing in the tilt of her head.

Through the fence, the Radcliffes began to shout. Valdez, the Radcliffe captain, yelled at Bucky to put his uniform back on.

Bucky took off his helmet and placed it on top of his jacket and shirt. He sat on his bike, bare-chested, grinning.

Valdez grabbed little Taylor and pulled her back so she couldn't start the race, causing the Skinners to jeer.

Bucky picked up his bottle, flipped it once in the air, caught it by the neck and began to pedal.

Gayle looked at her housemates, confused, angry. She grunted as she set off, shouting, 'Come on!' She swung the handlebars from side to side with the effort of breaking the bike's inertia. When the kids from Aleksanders realised Bucky wasn't going to stop, they roared like they'd never done before.

The sound of them, and of the fence bashing against its posts pumped Bucky up. The rough wall of the alley blurred as he pushed harder and faster.

He crossed into Gayle's side of the run. The distance closed between them, his pedals a blur. Nothing could stop him now, not breaking, not even leaping from his bike.

Gayle cocked her bottle-arm back and sunlight flared on the longest of its wicked points. Bucky threw his bottle to the ground. It exploded under his wheels. He grabbed both handlebars, put his head down, and pushed as hard as he could go.

If he was going to let Gayle sting him, it had to be hard enough that she'd never be able to sting him again.

Her bellow was bestial. Spit flew from her jaws. But Bucky had already won.

The Stone Thrower

HAL WAS AWAKENED by a brief expletive from one of the chickens outside. And then there was another, coupled with a dull thud. Out of bed, Hal stuck his head into the hoverfly graveyard between netting and pane to see that in the enclosure directly below the window, two of the chickens were dead.

And then a third fell. Right there as Hal watched. Something had shot down from the sky and smacked its head against the chicken wire, felling it with a squawk. A black pebble. The kind Maddy and his boys were collecting from the lake shore just yesterday, right outside the holiday house they'd fled to. Now, the other stones in the pen, the ones that had killed the first two chickens, were conspicuous beside them. Three stones, three dead chickens.

Hal followed the line of trajectory back, all the way across to the other side of the lake, where there was a person, a male, young. His white t-shirt was vivid against the dark wall of conifers behind as he curled his arm, winding himself up onto his back foot. He uncoiled with a co-ordinated swish that took in the whole of his body, terminating at his fingertips. The pebble he threw only became visible at the top of its arc, as it rounded against the brightening sky. Its descent was invisible, until it flared into being again, upon the head of chicken number four.

Now almost half the coop was killed.

These were not Hal's chickens, but while he rented the

house by the lake they were his charges. Indignation took him outside in his pyjamas, stopping only to plunge his feet into the still-damp boots that waited by the porch door.

'Oi!' he yelled, with his hands cupped either side of his mouth. 'What the hell are you doing?' The other side of the lake was far, five minutes in a rowing boat or a ten-minute walk round the side, too far to think about chasing the kid off.

Again the boy cocked his arm back and threw. Hal retreated to the porch, imagining what havoc a pebble lobbed with such force might wreak on his skull.

Hal heard the whistle of the stone displacing air as it shot into the coop and struck the back of chicken number five. The remaining four hopped up against the wire, all in the same corner, as if once there had been a door there.

Hal's binoculars were hanging on one of the hooks in the porch, alongside musty raincoats and propped oars. His hands shook as he looked through them, jiggling the image of the boy in the lenses. Hal did not feel the same sense of invisibility that he felt when watching the redstarts and flycatchers in the woods behind the house. Instead, he felt an increased sense of vulnerability, as if he were physically closer to the boy, and therefore an easier target – if there were such a thing as an easier target to this demon who'd felled five chickens with five stones from an impossible distance. Impossible, because Hal had thrown stones from the shore himself, with his boys, on several occasions over the last week. There'd been no attempts to throw stones to the other side because it was inconceivably far. They'd thrown only for the pleasure of throwing.

The boy looked only a year or two older than Joseph, the eldest of his boys, maybe 11 or 12. He moved with a disquieting confidence for a child. His hair was long at the front, a blonde fringe that hung over his right eye, all the way to his mouth. He stooped again, and the range of his spine stood out all the way down his back.

When he stood and threw, the thrust of his arm, the coiling and uncoiling of energy in his form, was breathtaking. Here was art. Prodigious skill, and in his face an Olympian's focus. Not the snarl Hal had expected, the kind of wonky facial arrangement that the local yahoos presented when they goaded him from the bus shelter on his trips to the chemist. This boy looked like a good boy. He was clean, and were he in a playing field hurling baseballs, his fringe tucked inside a cap, he would be a magnet for admiration.

The sixth chicken fell.

'For God's sake, will you stop!' he yelled from the porch. The force of the words drove spit from his lips. 'I have children in the house. I have a sick child. This isn't our house. These aren't my chickens.'

There were footsteps on the stairs, and then the inner door to the porch opened. It was Maddy in a pair of Hal's pyjamas.

'Get back upstairs!' Hal said. 'There's a crazy kid out here throwing stones.'

'Throwing stones?' Maddy came fully into the porch, rubbing the heel of her palm in her eye.

The seventh chicken was struck in such a way that a flurry of feathers sprang out from the point of impact on its lower back. Its last cluck was a wheeze.

Now the remaining two were hopping from one corner to the next, frantic, bobbing their heads forward, stepping round their fallen comrades.

'Don't go out there!' Maddy said as Hal flung open the door and bolted outside. Across the lake, the boy passed a pebble from right hand to left. Hal ran, and while he ran he threw his hands up into the air and called out 'Stop!' once again. But the boy did not stop.

'Get in here you idiot!' Maddy said, her head venturing no more than an inch or two outside. 'Have you called the police yet? I'm going to call the police.'

While Hal's fingers were on the latch of the coop, he

saw the boy throw. Hal flicked the metal hook from the eye. The chicken wire bit into his fingers as he lifted the door to swing it open. He scampered back to the house and was at the porch door when he turned and saw the eighth chicken fall, twitching. One of its legs kicked a regular beat in the dirt. It managed maybe ten of these kicks before a second stone struck its head, making its legs buck up off the ground.

'Is the number for the police still the same on a mobile?' Maddy said.

The boys were on the stairs now, and Maddy yelled at them, 'Get back in your room! Keep away from the windows!' But her panic brought smiles to their faces, widened their eyes, quickened their footsteps.

Hal barked with exasperation at the last chicken, whose timid evacuation of the cage was happening one slow strut at a time. Hal's shouts did nothing but force blinks out of its dumb face.

Again the boy stooped.

Hal ran out, leaping from side to side, corralling the chicken into the corner where the coop butted up against the house. Inside, Maddy held the boys back with her outstretched leg while she translated this event into terse statements of fact for the emergency services operator.

The back of Hal's neck prickled, sensitive to the stone's accelerating descent. He raked his fingers through the soft dirt and flung a handful of powdered soil and tiny stones to the left of the chicken, causing her to flap and flee, stranding herself in the corner, head pushed up against the house. And it was here that Hal seized her, throwing the whole length of himself into the dirt.

With the chicken squeezed between his two palms, he rolled onto his back, pivoted on his backside and was up and out of the way just as the stone hit the spot where he'd been less than a second ago and bounced up against the white-wood panels of the house.

Inside the safety of the porch, the boys were amazed at

the sight of a chicken alive indoors. Hal held it aloft, his pride immovable under the blizzard of Maddy's curses.

'Are the police on their way?' he asked.

'... Such a moron, thick as pig shit,' Maddy continued. 'Risking your life for a goddamned chicken. The boys and me alone in the house...'

'Who's out there Dad?' Joseph asked. 'Are the chickens really all dead?'

'All but this one,' Hal said, holding it up again. The chicken's neck was fully elongated, its head swivelling left and right, eyes rapid-blinking, camera shutters to take everything in. Hal looked out the window, at the boy across the lake, but only just glimpsed him walking away before the window exploded inwards.

The boys screamed. Something flashed across Hal's face. His whole world shattered into bright fragments. They were stunned by the sound of shards striking floortiles. Hands and arms flew up protectively, backs turned away from the window. There was blood. And all the while, he held the chicken high, his arms maintaining their stalwart position against the chaos.

Only when all the glass had fallen, and the clatter was ended, could Hal comprehend the scene. The faces of Maddy and both boys were spattered with blood. He felt something well up on his eyebrow and drip down onto his cheekbone. The chicken was decapitated, still kicking between his hands. Its blood ran down his arms, gathering at his elbows.

They were each stranded in a sea of glass, Maddy ordering them not to move, she and the boys barefoot. Their walking boots were cups for long and wicked splinters. Outside, the boy was gone.

Remember the Bride who Got Stung?

THEY'D ONLY BEEN walking for ten minutes, but already Victor was red and puffing. It was the fault of the picnic hamper that he was carrying. A real monster. Big enough to hold a body and so heavy that the leather handle had mangled his palm. Hefting it along the dirt track between the hedgerows and beneath the humming pylon cables, Victor could only take pigeon steps. His sandals kicked up dust clouds and sent little stones flying. There was no controlling this hamper. It had a will to swing in Victor's hand and he was powerless to stop it, even when it came for his shin with one of its pointy wicker corners.

Alerted by Victor's yelp, his wife and son, Tara and Nate, stopped and looked back.

'It's bloody lethal,' Victor said. He set down the hamper, lifting his leg to show Tara the bloody scrape. Now that he had stopped walking, his face leaked fresh sweat, heightening his skin's sensitivity to the faint breeze idling across the rape field.

'Nate just told me something very sad,' Tara said, making her baby face. When she pouted her lips like this it made Victor think of a cat's bottom.

'What's that?' Victor said, touching the edge of his wound and flinching.

'He said his imaginary friend died.'

Victor snorted. 'Oh dear,' he said. '*Quel dommage*. How did he die?'

'How did he die, pumpkin?' Tara asked.

'He killed himself,' Nate said.

'Oh for goodness' sake,' Victor said.

'What an *awful* thing to say,' Tara said. 'Why on *Earth...*'

'What's wrong with you?' Victor said.

Tara pushed her razor-straight fringe away from her forehead with both hands. She twisted the corner of her mouth to blow up onto her brow.

Nate picked at a scab on his elbow until Tara slapped the back of his hand. 'I keep telling you,' she said. Nate's bony knees, elbows and shins were all covered in the kind of pink skin you only find beneath scabs. He hooked one finger into the pocket of Tara's jeans. The hedgerows about them were dead silent.

Victor started to sit down on the edge of the hamper, till Tara stopped him with a single uttered syllable. 'Err!'

Victor rubbed his aching palm against his good one.

'We've got a way to go yet,' Tara said.

The wicker hamper groaned as Victor took up its weight again and followed behind them.

'Nate,' Victor said. 'Do you know how genuinely miserable some children in the world are? There are kids living in war zones who've seen soldiers shoot their parents. There are kids in third world villages without food and clean water. They don't have PlayStations. They have flies and diarrhoea.'

'We're about to eat,' Tara said.

'I just can't bear it,' Victor said. 'This *perpetual* gloom. You know, when there's a knock on the door now I'm terrified it's the bloody social worker.'

'You do over-dramatize,' Tara said.

Nate watched the ground as he walked. 'Head up,' Tara said.

'Is there an *actual* problem Nay-Nay?' Victor said. 'Because you know we can fix anything. Your mum and I are smarter than most parents, and you're better than both of us put together. There's no problem this world has to offer that we can't solve.'

Nate said nothing. He kicked a flint along in front of him.

This was the first time Victor had worn his shorts this year, and since last season he'd added a little girth to his thighs and belly, so when the phone buzzed in his pocket, he found it difficult to take out; so difficult that by the time it was free, his voicemail had got there before him.

'I thought you weren't working today,' Tara said.

'You're lucky I'm here at all,' Victor said. 'Dave's off sick and I've got two on leave, so there's only six today. I should be there. But I promised you, so I'm here. My phone may ring once or twice and I'll have to answer it. That's the situation.'

While Victor stopped to see who had called, Tara gained ground and practised Nate's French.

'*Ça va*?' she said.

'*Ça va mal*,' he replied.

'Oh Nay-Nay, why always *ça va mal*?'

The phone call had been from Steph, the longest-standing member of Victor's team, which made her the most senior at the orchards today.

'Sorry to bother you,' Steph said when he called her back, 'but he's insisting we're supposed to be pollinating all *six* orchards today.'

'Just tell him that's not what we agreed,' Victor said.

'But he keeps waving the order in front of my face. He keeps asking to speak to you,' she said.

'Don't give him my number. Just say that as far as you're aware, you're just pollinating four orchards today and you've only got the people to do four. Tell him if he keeps wasting your time going on about six you won't even have time to do four. But say it nicer than that. Just make sure you don't give him this number. I'm off the radar today.'

'He's not happy.'

'Just claim ignorance and tell him I'll be back tonight to straighten it all out.'

All the way through the fields, over the hill and then down the other side, was a small wooded area. Here in the luxurious shade of the trees, Victor stopped to take a bottle of water from the hamper. He should have drunk 20 minutes ago when thirst had first played on his tongue. Now, in the heat, with the sweating and the strain of carrying Tara's new hamper, a headache was announcing itself in his temples. He took a few mouthfuls, then wiped his palm over the bottle's chilled surface and applied the condensation to his face.

'Honey, remember we're going to have to walk the whole way back too,' Victor called after Tara.

'Oh shut up,' she said. 'We're almost there.'

'Anywhere here would be lovely, don't you think?'

Tara ignored him and carried on. It was 1:45pm, already way past lunchtime.

Deep into the wooded area, a steep bank dropped down from the left side of the path, and from the bottom of it came the sound of running water. Victor could not see the stream because metre-high ferns covered everything, but the sound alone had a restorative effect that allowed him to walk faster and catch up with Tara and Nate. Only when this sound was far behind them did they reach the little archway of trees that led out into Tara's glade.

The feathery grasses here were so tall that Victor had to walk back and forth over an area to flatten it enough to lay down a blanket. And before they could sit on it, they all had to march about the blanket on their fists and knees to break the stubborn stems beneath.

'I can't believe there's not a closer parking space,' Victor said.

'When we used to come here,' Tara said, 'that car park

was always full, and you'd get cars parked up the verges the whole way along the road. One time, Nay, your grandpa parked on a verge that was so steep the car almost rolled over with us all in it. I can't believe how quiet it is now.'

'Well, it's a nice spot,' Victor said. 'Once you get here.'

He flopped onto his side. The sun-warmed blanket was a great comfort to his aches. With his eyes closed he could just about hear the drone of the motorway a couple of miles away, before it was obliterated by Tara opening the hamper's creaky lid, tearing plastic wrappings from the baguette and tomatoes, and popping the vacuum seals of Tupperware boxes.

'You know,' Victor said, 'you can almost imagine that we're the last people on earth.' As if to contradict him, the phone in his pocket buzzed again.

'If you answer that,' Tara said, 'I'm packing up and we're all going home.'

'Don't be so ridiculous,' Victor said, rolling onto his back so his fingers could access the tight pocket. He got up and answered the phone, heading back towards the path and shade. But before he got there, he stopped.

'He what!' he said.

'He told us to go away and come back when we're ready to do six orchards,' Steph said. 'He's mad.'

'Well what did you say to him?'

'Nothing!'

'Where are you now?'

'We're just getting in the van. I can still see him. Do you want to speak to him?'

'Not now. Jesus. Look I'll…' and then, for the first time ever, Victor hung up on her. Regret came instantly and held him there for a moment. He stared at the still tops of the tall grasses, little flies in dogfights, and high above, wispy cirrus clouds bleeding streaks of ice. He cursed it all.

Back at the blanket, Tara was smearing houmous over a lump of French bread with the back of a spoon.

'Can you switch it off now?' she said.

'Why don't you use a knife?' Victor asked, pushing the phone back into his pocket.

'You didn't pack one.'

'I clearly remember putting it in.'

'Well, between that moment and this, it's gone missing.'

Victor rummaged in the hamper, feeling inside the red canvas pockets but found no knife except his Leatherman.

'So will you turn off your phone now so we can have lunch in peace?' Tara said.

'You know I can't, but she won't call again now. I had to lie to a good customer to be here today, so you can at least be a little bit grateful.'

'We are grateful, aren't we Nay-Nay,' she said, sinking a black olive into the thick houmous and then passing it to Nate. 'We're very grateful.'

Victor cut off a long piece of baguette with the Leatherman. The sharp blade went through it in a couple of easy strokes. Holding the bread in his hand, he sliced along its length, being careful to stop the blade before it got close to his palm. He wiped the knife on his hip, folded the blade away, then peeled open the pack of salami and stuffed five slices inside the bread. 'Meat,' he said, in his deepest voice.

Using Tara's spoon, he scooped a great dollop of houmous into the sandwich and spread it around. When he took his first bite, the houmous leaked out the side and needed licking away.

'Ahhhhhh,' he groaned, closing his eyes. 'It's amazing how good simple food tastes after an hour of pain.'

'You do exaggerate.'

Victor's enthusiasm for his sandwich left him breathless. 'Now, Nate,' he said, caching his mouthful in his cheek. 'This imaginary friend of yours. Is he gone forever, or can you bring him back to life somehow?'

'Not now,' Tara said.

'It's a serious question…'

'Not today.'

'You're right. I'm sorry. This is your special day.'

'This *is* a special day for Mummy,' she said, screwing the top back on the apple juice. 'If your granddad were still alive, Nay, he would have been seventy today. Do you remember your granddad?'

Nate squeezed his lips into a thinking shape and nodded.

'When I was your age, my parents used to bring me and your aunties here all the time, and our cousins. I don't think you've ever met them. We'd have a big group of us, seven children, and three blankets all joined together. My parents didn't have any money for fancy picnics like this, so we just had marmite sandwiches and apples, but it was so good. And when all the grown ups were having a sleep in the afternoon, we'd go down to the little stream over there and catch freshwater shrimp in crisp packets. We used to pretend they were seahorses. We'll go exploring after we've eaten, and see if it's still there.' All the while Tara talked, her smile widened. But then she stopped suddenly and her face dropped back to its default setting. 'Victor,' she said. 'Is that your phone *again*?'

Victor had felt no vibration, but took out his phone to check.

'No,' he said.

But there *was* a buzzing sound.

'It sounds like a bee,' Tara said.

'It can't be.'

But then, there it was, however improbable. A honey bee. Just like the bees Victor remembered from his youth. Its appearance between them caused both Victor and Tara to leap up and draw their heads back to the full extent of their necks to distance themselves from it. Nate jumped up too, arms wrapped round himself for protection.

Victor looked around the blanket for a weapon. 'Give me something to hit it with,' he said.

'No!' Tara said. 'You'll make it angry.'

The distance between the three of them widened as each backed away from its advances. The bee expanded the zone of its patrol until it claimed the whole airspace above the blanket as its own. It amplified its buzz as it flew at each of them, performing a triangular attack pattern that caused them to shriek when it came near.

They were pushed back to a distance where they needed to shout to communicate with each other. The beast teased them for a minute more, before swooping down onto the pale skin of Nate's bare shin.

Nate's hysteria was so fully brewed by now that he heeded none of Victor or Tara's contradictory instructions and swatted it with his hand.

Victor and Tara ran to him, their speed accelerated by his explosive yell of 'Ow!'

'Show me!' Tara said, trying to pull his hands away, but Nate resisted.

'Let us see,' Victor said.

'No!' Nate said. 'It hurts. It hurts really bad.'

Victor wrapped his hairy fingers round Nate's wrist and pulled it away so he could get a good look. Nate's other arm was around his mother's neck. He hopped on one foot, holding the stung leg aloft.

'Keep still a second,' Victor said, putting one hand under Nate's knee to hold it steady.

On the front of Nate's shin, the small brown lance of the bee's sting was still sunk into his skin. At the end of it was a butter-yellow glob of goo. Tara leaned in closer and said, 'Good God it's still pulsing!' She smacked it with her fingers till it was gone, leaving behind a fierce red dot surrounded by a ring of pale swollen skin.

'Please tell me you brought the syringe?' Tara said.

'Where the hell did a bee come from!?' Victor said.

'Did you bring the syringe?!' she said again.

'When was the last time we needed it!'

'We have to take it everywhere!'

'Well, we always kept it in the old hamper, but now we've got your new one.'

'Well why didn't you transfer it over?'

'I wasn't the only one who did the packing!'

Victor shifted his weight from foot to foot, looking from the wound to the direction of the car.

'How long does it...?' Victor said.

'I don't know!' she hissed, 'And be careful what you say, don't make it worse! Pick him up, we have to run.'

'It took us an hour to get here. And even when we get to the car, do you know where the nearest hospital is?'

'Why didn't we pack the damn syringe!!'

Nate's tears were flowing readily now. He forced noisy breaths through his teeth. 'It hurts!' he said.

'It's okay honey,' Tara said. 'Just relax. Everything's okay. It's just a sting.'

As soon as Tara had named it 'a sting', Nate's howling doubled in volume.

'We have to move!' Tara said.

'Wait,' Victor said, his fingertips on his temples. 'Remember the bride who got stung on her way to the church?'

'What bride?'

'The story, you told me, you read it in a magazine somewhere. The bride got stung on her way to the church and she was allergic and she didn't have her shot with her, but she was so nervous about the wedding she had already pumped herself full of adrenaline, so she survived.'

'Victor, we need to go.'

'No, this is the only thing to do.'

'What is?'

Victor knelt down beside Nate and put his arm around his waist.

'Nay-Nay,' Victor said. 'I'm going to be honest with you. This is bad. Do you remember how we always said when you were little, if you ever happened to see a bee, to keep away from it?'

'What are you doing?' Tara said, brushing hair from her sticky face. 'Pick him up. We have to hurry.'

'You're allergic to stings,' Victor said. '*Very* allergic. So we've got two choices. We can make a run for the car together and try to find the nearest hospital, but there's a good chance we won't get there in time, or...'

'Good God Victor! Shut up! Here I'll pick him up.' Tara bent low to scoop her hands under his legs, but Victor barred her way with his outstretched hand.

'There isn't time,' he said. 'Our other option poppet, is to deal with the poison in your leg before it gets any further into your body. If we do it now we might just catch it.'

'You can't suck out bee poison!' Tara said.

'No we can't suck it out. We're going to have to do something more drastic, and you're going to have to be brave Nate, because this is going to hurt.'

Tightening his right arm around Nate's waist to hold him firm, Victor reached down with his left hand and picked up the Leatherman knife from the blanket.

'No way! *No* way!' Nate yelled, using both hands to push against the side of Victor's face.

'Get off him! What the hell's wrong with you!' Tara's shout filled the whole clearing. She grabbed Nate under his arms and tried to pull him away, but Victor's grip was solid.

'It's the only way! We have to do it now!' Victor winked at her, but she was blind to it, still trying to pull Nate from him. 'You have to help Ta. Come on, remember the bride and the bee. We've got no choice!' Victor wrapped both his arms round Nate's waist and pushed Tara away with his foot. She fell on her bottom. Nate scratched Victor's face, raking up sore streaks. 'I'm trying to save your life!' Victor said.

'Victor for fuck's sake!' Tara howled as she got up.

Nate fought his way to his feet, but Victor tackled him

down on the ground again. Thick grass stems jabbed into his side where his polo shirt had ridden all the way up to his armpits. His face was throbbing, especially his left eyelid which he couldn't open properly.

Nate screamed into Victor's ear. Tara kicked his back, and when she saw him dig his thumbnail into the groove of the blade and pull out the bright length of it, she grabbed him round the throat and squeezed.

'Get off him!' she said. 'What's wrong with you?!'

'For God's sake woman,' he gurgled. '*Play along*!'

Victor leaned on Nate's stomach and pinned his ankles down with one foot. He put the blade against Nate's skin, just below the knee. Nate hit the back of Victor's head and scratched his neck, bawling all the while.

'Hold still!' Victor said.

Something sharp jabbed into Victor's right eye and it filled up with tears. 'I can't see!' he yelled. 'You've fucking blinded me!' Victor dropped the knife and put his hands to his eye.

Nate pummelled Victor with his knees, elbows and knuckles, scrambling to get free of his father's weight. Tara grabbed Nate's wrists and helped him out, lifting him to his feet. Together they fled through the long grass.

'I'm pretending you stupid fuck! I'm pretending!'

Victor rolled onto his back, heaving for breath. The ring of trees in the clearing was a blurry mess to his scratched eyes. Welts rose all over his face and neck. His lips were too tender to touch with his tongue. 'I was pretending,' he said again.

Tara and Nate's fleeing footsteps cracked twigs at the edge of the glade. They were moving fast. Victor winced, wondering if he'd done too much, if he'd done enough.

An Industrial Evolution

'I am jostling for position, trying to find a view in the gaps between elbows and bodies. I cannot miss it. This moment. Ellie gasps and grunts and groans. One of the surgeons shifts, and then… there it is. Pulled from her roughly, it seems to me, its orange fur dark and slicked down against its tiny frame. The world has just become a different place. Another genie is out of the bottle.'

Caspar Stak, *Black Window*, June 2024 Issue.

EVEN THOUGH THE road from Kapas to Perjan Tungul is now so smooth that the bus glides with barely a bump, ten minutes into our journey a man in the back row gets travelsick and lays a Duty Free carrier bag on the floor to cover it. I spend the next four hours with a t-shirt tied round my face, my headphones in, and my eyes closed.

I arrive just after three in the afternoon, and am surprised to see here a big café with parasols, cushions on the chairs, waiters in white shirts, a fountain, and a bar made entirely from glass with an enormous fruit and flower arrangement in the centre. This is not the Sumatra I remember.

To step out of the bus, I must break through a wall of heat. It seems to roar in my ears. Eleanor has arrived on an earlier bus, and is sitting on her suitcase in the shade of a palm tree. Three young boys crowd her knees. All four are talking and laughing.

It has been 20 years since I saw her, and even though she

has aged considerably during her exile in Canada, she is instantly recognisable: the conspiratorial hunch and sideways tilt of the head, the nodding, the emphatic hand wringing. Like her beloved orangutans, she is thick in body and long in limb. Her hair a comb-shy tangle of white weeds.

I can delay this moment no longer.

Eleanor doesn't notice me, or doesn't appear to, until I'm right by her side when, making a demonic shape of her face, she says to the children, 'This is one of the most evil men in the world. Don't even look at him. It will bring you nothing but misery.'

The boat we take is a public transit, holding about 20 people, and depositing them one or two at a time on the jetties that poke out of the riverbanks like a parade of eager tongues. Banau Batong is the last stop, more than an hour on from the penultimate drop off, and we are the only ones travelling there. Eleanor sits in the front of the boat, chatting with the captain, he letting her steer where the brown river runs straight. She has one leg crossed over the other, and has let her sandals slip off. The soles of her feet are leather, her toenails turquoise.

I sit at the back, in the panel of sunshine, growing giddy on the nostalgic pleasure of petrol fumes, enjoying the sun against my closed eyelids, listening to the engine, the water sloshing against the hull, and the few bird calls. When I made this journey, aged 23, I was enthusiastically pointing my phone this way and that, trying to film the gaudy sunbirds that flashed between the trees, and the crocs that crossed the river like zippers. I had wanted to capture the sounds, so I could spend time back at my desk in England describing faithfully the thrum of life, intoxicating in its richness, an aural assault from 10,000 throats and stridulating insect legs. Now, the sense of loneliness here is so eerie, I give up the sun to move to the front of the boat and sit on the cushioned bench close to the captain and Eleanor.

'It was a good idea to take the scenic route,' I say.

Eleanor nods.

'It's so quiet though,' I say, 'isn't it?'

Eleanor raises her eyebrows. She has the most remarkable eyes. Amber, flecked with gold. A toad's eyes. Quite beautiful.

'I barely recognise it,' I continue. 'It must be even stranger for you.'

She licks her lips. 'Strange is what used to make this place special. Now it's…'

She stares at the ripples we leave behind us, maybe searching for the right word, but doesn't find it.

The Banau Batong base camp is surrounded by a moat. A slimy green mosquito nursery. A man is painting the wooden drawbridge that crosses it white. On the end of the bridge closest to us, there is an orangutan. This limp-limbed wookie is the first I've seen in 20 years, but unlike any I've ever seen.

The orang is standing upright, leaning on the wooden rail looking down into the moat. He is wearing a pair of cut off denim shorts, and a baggy yellow t-shirt that has a bib of berry stains and is stretched long around the neck. He has on a red baseball cap with the Banau Batong company logo – two black B's placed back to back, like a butterfly.

'Is it safe to cross?' I call to the man, pointing at the orang.

The man seems puzzled. He gestures with a sweep of his paintbrush in the air that it's okay to go.

Eleanor has already taken the initiative and is walking towards the ape with a kind of droopy body posture and her head flopped down, chin almost on her chest. The man stops painting to watch as she gets closer. The orang turns his glassy black eyes to her, then gives an eerily human upwards nod in greeting, and holds his fist out towards her.

Eleanor is confused. She looks across at the man, who

smiles and comes over to demonstrate what we should do. He holds out his own fist and gently knocks knuckles with the orang.

'This is Homer,' he says.

Homer, we are soon to see, is not unusual here.

Basecamp is a village of wooden cabins on short stilts, home to almost 60 workers and their families. When we arrive, most of them are out on the plantation, and the place feels deserted, but there are three old men on foldaway seats watching a Brazil versus Argentina match on a huge screen on the side of the largest building. Above them looms a water tower, and painted on its side is a cartoon orangutan face.

We are met here by Adhi Perkasa, the Banau Batong Manager. He wears chinos, a pink polo shirt, white leather shoes and a white flat cap. I am relieved that his English is quite good, and that he seems pleased to see us. He gives me a two-handed handshake, and then kisses Eleanor on the cheek – it leads me to suspect that he doesn't realise who she is.

It is now 6pm, and the humidity has turned the air to soup. Grey-brown clouds churn above us. There is nothing I want more than for them to break so I can stand here and rinse off the last 48 hours. They rumble, teasingly.

Adhi takes us to the cabins where we'll be staying, on the way explaining that he has worked at Banau Batong since he was 16, working his way up through the ranks of harvesters and supervisor levels. He is now 29 and manages the whole plantation, an area of more than 90,000 hectares. This is the third largest oil palm plantation in Sumatra.

'A big responsibility,' I say. He raps on his chest with the side of his thumb, and gives a confident wink.

Two young girls, both wearing baggy dresses cut from the same floral fabric, run to him, calling out 'Adhi! Adhi!' and stretch up to slap his slightly protuberant belly, demanding sweets. He pinches both of their noses, and then reaches into his pocket and takes out two hard-boiled mints in plastic wrappers.

'How many orangutans do you have here?' Eleanor asks.

Adhi looks confused. '*These* are not orangutans,' he says, ruffling the girls' hair. 'These are our *children*.' He pauses a moment before breaking into a big laugh that exposes the whole cavern of his mouth and all of his bright teeth.

Eleanor and I have our own cabin with adjoining rooms. The rooms are small, but surprisingly well kitted-out. I have a big plush bed, and the curtains match the bedspread – a tasteful pattern of overlapping orange, white and red circles. When Banau Batong was still a rainforest reserve, I had to share a shed with two volunteers and a pink tarantula, and I slept on a stinky camp bed.

'There's an insectocutor!' I note with delight. 'I was dreading getting eaten alive again.'

'We look after you,' Adhi says.

Eleanor and I are to share a bathroom that is sandwiched between our rooms. I notice that neither door to the bathroom has a lock.

'We'll have to whistle when we're in there,' I say.

'I can't whistle,' Eleanor says. 'But if you open the door while I'm in there, I'll scream.'

Adhi loves this. 'She'll scream,' he says, thumping me on the chest with the back of his hand. Even as he leaves us alone to unpack, he is still laughing about this. 'She scream!'

We eat dinner in a big dining hall with the workers and their families. I'd been hoping there would be lots of orangutans at the base camp, but Adhi tells us Homer is the only ape that lives away from the main colony, a kind of mascot.

'I take him from poachers when he was a baby,' Adhi says. 'My father was a boxer. He teaches me.'

Adhi's father was one of 14 people killed trying to

control a fire that ripped through part of Banau Batong ten years ago. High up on the wall behind the serving counter, there's a memorial collage of these people made from leaves and seeds.

The residents of Banau Batong bash elbows as they eat, talking over the top of each other. Their children sit on the tables, under the tables, run between the tables. The air conditioning in this room is set high and I am now kicking myself for not bringing a jumper.

I wish that I spoke a little of the language. My ignorance excludes me from most of the conversations. Eleanor's tongue finds the words she hasn't spoken for 15 years as if it were only 15 days.

Dinner is fried tofu with sticky rice, shredded cucumber and a spicy peanut sauce.

'You like it?' Adhi asks.

'It's actually really good,' I say. He smiles and pats me on the back. When I've finished, he says I should follow him to the kitchen. Here, the larder shelves are stacked with hundreds of plastic gallon-bottles of dark red palm oil, all bearing the Banau Batong label – the same cartoon orangutan that is painted on the water tower.

'We have this in England, too,' I say. 'You can't eat or wash without using something that has this in the ingredients.'

Adhi looks genuinely moved by this.

On the first night, Eleanor and I slump in canvas deck chairs beside a fire in a metal drum. Above us is the big screen, which is now showing tennis. The clouds continue to rumble overhead but do not break. My eyes are stinging because I sprayed too much mosquito repellent on my face. It makes every sip of beer taste a little bit like lemon, and a little bit like poison. The repellent was not even necessary, as I've now noticed insectocutors, like blue lanterns, on every post around the moat.

'I was surprised when my editor said you'd agreed to come back,' I say. 'Pleasantly surprised, I mean.'

'I nearly didn't.'

'Well, I'm glad you did.'

She stares at me, maybe wondering if I'm being serious.

'My little girl begged me not to come,' I say. 'She's inherited a fear of planes from her mum.'

'I didn't know you had children,' Eleanor says.

'Just Hattie, she's eight.'

'That's nice.'

'How is Michael?'

She shrugs.

'How long has it been?' I ask.

'Even when I left a voicemail about my cancer he wouldn't call.'

'I didn't know. Is it… one of the bad ones?'

'I've already had it chopped off,' she says, indelicately flipping her remaining boob up from underneath. 'They caught it in time.'

'I'm so sorry.'

'Cancer's one thing you're not responsible for.'

We don't say anything else for a long time, but just sit there and listen to a far away radio playing the Rolling Stones' *Paint it Black*, and to the riot of cicadas – about the only wildlife that remains here in profusion. I'm exhausted after the two days' travelling, but I don't want to leave Eleanor out here alone. She sits there for so long, unmoving, that eventually I can't bear it any longer. I'm about to say that I have to go to bed when she starts snoring. I crouch beside her and gently shake her arm. She wakes with a violent start, horrified to see my face so close.

The storm breaks during the night. Thunder and rain make a warzone of my dreams, and I wake exhausted.

Breakfast is rice with curried vegetables and a fried egg

on top. Eleanor and I shovel the food into our mouths, both of us eager to get our first glimpse of the plantation, and especially the apes. Adhi takes us in a brand-new chilli-red jeep. He proudly strokes the cream leather upholstery and the glossy walnut dash. 'It's a work of art,' I say, and this pleases him. The road through the plantation is so straight and flat that he has all the control of the jeep he needs with just one finger on the steering wheel.

The scale of the plantation is terrifying. We drive for maybe an hour before we reach the area where harvesting is happening today, a whole hour of exactly the same view, unchanging, identical tree after identical tree, perfectly spaced apart. It has a hypnotic effect, which seems to dilate time and make this journey torturous.

Finally, mercifully, I see an orangutan dragging a palm leaf across the orange dirt. 'I see one!' I call out, the way I used to call out 'I see the sea!' on trips to the beach. And then there are more. Lots more. Dozens of them.

'Exactly how many orangs do you have here?' Eleanor asks as Adhi stops the jeep.

'Exactly is not possible to say,' he says. 'Maybe, in whole plantation, seven, eight hundred.'

Eleanor's mouth drops open. At the peak of her orangutan reserve, she had around 90 apes, and they were spread over an area half the size of Greater London. Here, in ten times the number, and all working within a square mile, the sight is overwhelming. Beneath the canopy of palm fronds, the air is filled with the sound of their soft-hoot conversations and the hum of the buzz scythes that they wield. These industrious orange apes lurch to and fro, a sense of orderliness to their activities. There is co-ordination, co-operation. This is a factory floor, a production line, each ape engaged in his or her task but mindful of its neighbours, constantly reassuring each other with nods and an incredible array of elastic expressions.

The orangs all wear clothes, even the young ones

clinging to their mothers' stomachs while they work, t-shirts at least – most of them orange and bearing the Banau Batong logo. It's easy to tell how old the orangs are, relative to each other, from the colour of their t-shirts. The older the ape, the more the sun has bleached the dye.

They all walk upright, lumbering in a kind of drunken way that makes the hairs on the back of my arms stand up, because most of them are carrying highly dangerous tools.

Adhi makes a 'give me' gesture, and the orang nearest us gives up his buzz scythe. This is a seven-foot pole with a wicked-sharp sickle on the end that vibrates when a button on the handle is pressed.

'When my grandfather worked in the plantation,' he says, 'he had a long pole with flat blade and he have to jab jab jab at each leaf to prune the tree, then jab jab jab, ten times for each fruit. It takes him 15 minutes to harvest one tree. Now…'

He gives the buzz scythe back to the orang and makes a gesture, clapping his fingers against his thumb.

'How many sign words do they know?' Eleanor asks.

Adhi shrugs. 'We have signs for everything we need to say.'

The orang responds by going at the tree with quick, accurate pulling motions, hooking the scythe round the thick stem of each leaf and pruning it away to reveal the red fruit balls that sprout from the top of the trunk like monstrous half-metre raspberries. The ape chops seven leaves in 30 seconds, then severs the short stem of the first fruit. While we have watched this, another orang has come over to stand at the base of the tree. It seems to practise the act of catching a couple of times in the air, and when the actual fruit topples, it clutches the heavy ball against its chest, wrapping its impossibly long arms around it, then sets the fruit gently on the ground and waits for the next one to fall.

'Before apes,' Adhi says, 'the workers let fruit hit the ground. They get bruised. We lose many fruit this way. Now, all is perfect.' He grins proudly and pinches his thumb and forefinger together to make a loop. The universal symbol of perfection.

Working together, these two apes strip the tree down to a bare nub, pile the six fruits in one of the many trailers, and stack the discarded pine fronds in a cage, all within about three minutes. Adhi says the trucks take the fruits to a processing factory at the northern edge of the plantation.

'Are they engineered to be like this?' I ask. 'You know, so dextrous?'

Adhi doesn't understand, but Eleanor interprets, and he responds in English that they are 'normal apes'.

'At the centre,' Eleanor says, 'we always had to be careful about the behaviours the orangs picked up from us, so they could still act like wild apes when we released them onto the reserve. The orangs were always inquisitive about what we were doing, but these apes here, this is…'

'It's amazing,' I say.

Eleanor looks sour. 'Is that what you're going to write in your article, that this place is AMAZING?'

'We don't teach them,' Adhi says, 'they teach each other.'

'Monkey see monkey do,' I say, and Adhi laughs.

'Those cutting tools look very dangerous,' Eleanor says. 'How do you ensure the orangutans' safety?'

'We have ape hospital,' Adhi says.

Eleanor and I both want to see where the orangutans live – Ape Town, as Adhi calls it – but he insists that there isn't enough time, and the apes won't be there now anyway. He promises to take us there tomorrow. I sleep most of the drive back, and wake to a fire-gold sunset so beautiful I send my wife and daughter a picture, along with one of the shots I took of an orang with a buzz scythe, and one of my tired face, with the message, 'Perfect sunset. Clever monkey. I am miserable without you.'

After a long hot shower, I go to the dining hall for

dinner. Eleanor is already there with Adhi. Tonight, dinner is a prawn curry that is so hot I sniff all the way through it. A teenage girl sitting beside me takes a hard-bound sketchbook from her canvas bag, and a little hand-stitched roll of pencils. She draws me in profile, licking the tip of her finger to smudge the soluble graphite, and complains whenever I turn my head and talk. I am a disobedient model for maybe 15 minutes, during which I discover that her name is Ndari, she was born in Banau Batong, that her father was also one of the men killed in the great fire of 2034, and her ambition is to work on a ship. Nothing specific. Just any kind of work on a ship. Her drawing is not flattering, but her sketches of the orangutans are something else. I ask if I can buy one, a portrait of an old female that must have taken her hours. She tears it out of the book and refuses payment. So wrapped up am I in this sketch and questioning Ndari about her terrific gift that I miss the beginning of an argument between Eleanor and Adhi. I only become aware of it when I see at the edge of my vision Eleanor waving a dirty spoon at him in a threatening manner.

'Come in my office,' Adhi says to her. 'I'll show you my prizes.'

'I don't want to go in your office,' she says. 'They're obviously idiots. You've not *saved* anything. You've ruined them.'

'To be fair,' I say, picking up the gist of the conversation, 'these apes were never *purely* wild. Most of them will be descended from your apes, won't they?'

Eleanor flushes white. I realise too late that maybe I shouldn't have said that.

'What?' Adhi says. 'You're Ellie *Lundgren*?' He laughs out loud, claps his hands together, addresses the rest of our table in Indonesian, points at her. There is laughter that spreads infectiously. Her surname passes from mouth to mouth. Soon it seems the whole room is in hysterics, wiping coffee from their chins with the backs of their hands. It is a loud and ugly sound that drives Eleanor from the room, slamming the door shut behind her.

I leave shortly afterwards. Heading back to my cabin, I see Eleanor outside with Homer the orangutan, helping him fill a tin cup from a tap on the side of the building. The news is on the big screen, shining blue light onto them, but no one is watching it. This TV stays on all day and all night, the fire that never goes out.

I know I should go and apologise, but this moment doesn't feel like the right one.

Back in my cabin, I try making some notes but cannot concentrate, so I stop and put my head on the pillow, leaving the lamp on. After an hour or so of restlessness, I hear Eleanor brushing her teeth in the bathroom. I get up and knock on the door.

'I'm sorry,' I say to the closed door. 'You know, the whole reason I agreed to do this article was to try to make up for whatever part I played in how everything went before. I guess I'm failing at that.'

The bathroom door opens, and Eleanor is wearing a tight-fitting long-sleeved t-shirt tucked into some kind of long-johns, which are tucked into her socks. She has a toothbrush clamped in her mouth, and a little white foam on her knuckles.

'This really isn't all about you,' she says. Flecks of foam fly in my direction.

'Why *did* you agree to come back?' I ask.

'It was a mistake.'

The door behind her opens and Homer stands there looking into the cabin, silhouetted by the bright light outside. His shaggy fur makes a brilliant orange aura. 'Off you shoo you big brute,' she says, but he is reluctant and takes some physical pushing.

I tell her to lock her door, and she scoffs at this.

'These aren't the apes you used to know,' I say.

A few minutes later, when I'm lying in bed, I hear the click of her door lock.

We have to set out for Ape Town at 4am. Adhi says that at 7am, all the trucks arrive to take the orangs out to whichever part of the plantation they'll be working.

'Today we see your babies Ellie,' Adhi says, making his characteristic belly laugh that after 36 hours here is grating.

'Be kind,' I tell him, and he smiles, holding up his hands and bowing his head a little in deference.

Again the drive is long, 90 minutes through dismal monoculture. Every hour I spend here, the monotony of it depletes me a little more. My eyes ache for variety.

In my imagination, Ape Town would be a shanty town, reeking of garbage, the apes bundled together in nests they'd crudely constructed from the detritus of the palm oil industry. As we reach the outskirts, I realise how wrong I am.

The sun is just rising, and against the yellow sky are hundreds of cabins on stilts in long straight lines. Row after row of them. Adhi drives slowly through this grid of open-front cabins. Eleanor and I wind down our windows and hear the most extraordinary sound, the accumulated sleep noises of 800 apes. It's like purring, like an old engine, like something bubbling up from underground.

In each of the cabins, sleeping orangs are heaped together. It is impossible to say how many are in each one, so enfolded are they, but I would guess at about four or five. Sleepy faces turn towards us. They make enormous yawns, stretch their long arms, shuffle for comfort and settle again.

'There are males there too,' Eleanor whispers.

'They all sleep like this,' Adhi says.

I ask what the significance of this is, and Eleanor says that in the wild, orangs didn't form groups. Young apes stayed with their mothers for eight years until maturity, but the males were absent wanderers, seeking the company of females only to mate, occasionally fighting with another male for territory.

'What about the senior males?' Eleanor asks.

'No top apes,' Adhi says. 'Listen, you will hear.'

We're all quiet for a moment. From far away, we hear a series of drawn-out throaty calls. This, I come to understand, is a recording of an alpha male. The sound inhibits the release of hormones in the males, keeping them subservient to this facsimile ape, and even stops their wide cheek flanges from developing. This is not a trait that has been engineered into these clones. Adhi is simply utilising a natural tendency within the apes.

'There's nowhere for them to climb,' Eleanor says.

'They don't like to climb so much.'

'You've got a hell of a set up here,' I say.

With her fingertips, Eleanor rubs her temples, her eyes, and then her whole face with both hands.

The hospital is a big wooden building at the edge of Ape Town. Like the base camp, it is surrounded by a moat and connected to the mainland by a drawbridge.

A young woman wearing khaki shorts, white linen shirt and green wellington boots comes out to greet us. Her hand is soft and sticky. She looks harassed, but happy to see us. Her name is Mariana. Originally from Brazil, she has worked at the Banau Batong ape hospital for two years now, managing a team of just two nurses. She shows us round the four wide rooms that comprise the treatment centre. This place reminds me of a children's A&E department. Plastic boxes of toys are stacked up against the walls. Simple clouds are painted on the ceiling. Hanging in canvas sorters designed for shoes are vacuum-sealed packs of medical paraphernalia – bandaging, scissors, plastic devices the purpose of which I cannot guess. The whole place smells of pine.

On the day that we visit, there are 17 orangs in the hospital with a mixture of maladies and injuries all the way from flu to severed limbs. On a blanket on the floor of one room is a young male ape called Lennie who flicks through a children's board book with his one long arm. The other arm terminates before the elbow in a bulge of bandage.

A female ape totters through the doorway (again walking on two feet – I've yet to see a single dragged knuckle) and holds out her arms to demand a hug, which Mariana readily gives her. 'This is Bonnie,' Mariana says. 'She's going to be a mommie, aren't you Bonnie?'

Eleanor gasps, and kneels down to hold Bonnie's hand. I feel silly for not noticing the ape's enormous pregnancy bulge right away.

'She's so *young*,' Eleanor says.

'She's eleven. We find eleven to thirteen is about average here,' Mariana says.

'My goodness, and how long in between births?'

'Usually three years.'

'*Three*?' Eleanor says.

'Why the speed up?' I ask. When Banau Batong was seized by officials, and Eleanor dragged in front of the ethics panel, she insisted she'd had to breach the conditions of her cloning permit, and risk her own life, because of the eight-year gap between orangutan pregnancies. If she hadn't, the last few orangs would have died nearly two decades ago. This is a fact.

'We're not sure,' Mariana says, 'but it may be because they don't have to face the same challenges that a true wild ape would have.'

'Do you have any young ones here?' Eleanor asks.

'Oh yes,' Mariana smiles. 'Our nursery is through here.'

Eleanor comes to life in the nursery, as soon as she sees the little ones, three of them, sat on a fleece jumper in a wooden crate together. And they *are* impossibly cute. Their big black eyes and their dopey wide grins. Their wild orange hair that sticks up all over the place. Their lovely fat bellies. Their comical inquisitiveness. Cute in a way that makes human babies look boring. They are utterly adorable, and even I am down on my knees holding out a finger for one of the three to grip.

Eleanor coos over them, blowing their faces, and they love it, closing their eyes and wobbling. Eleanor asks Mariana a stream of questions about their care, about their mothers, about how long they spend socialising with mature apes, their diet, weight and whatnot, but I barely listen because one of these gorgeous little things has crawled onto my lap and is hugging me and I am giggling, enchanted.

We eat wedges of pineapple for lunch, flatbread and tall glasses of rice milk. Afterwards, Eleanor stays inside while Adhi and I walk the perimeter of the moat. We absently begin kicking an orange forward whenever we come to it again, and soon we organize ourselves into taking turns, passing it from one to the other.

I ask him about the future of the Banau Batong project. The ape population here now outnumbers the human population eight to one. It's hugely successful. Where does he go from here?

'Forty years ago, there were seven thousand orangutan in Sumatra,' he says. 'Now about eight hundred. We have a long way to go.'

'So Ape Town will continue to grow, with more orangs working in the plantation every year?'

'It is early days,' he says. 'But apes make good economy. They eat small. They like work. They make no complaint. What we have here, other places can have. Everyone profits.'

'Franchising?' I say.

Adhi smiles and raps the side of his thumb against his chest.

When we've finished a full loop of the moat, and Adhi has kicked the orange into the water, it is time to go. Eleanor and Mariana are outside. They have all three baby chimps in a half-barrel filled with soapy water, and are making hats and beards on the babies with bubbles. The orangs' fur is flattened against their bodies. One of the apes slaps both hands into the water, sloshing a wave over the edge and right into Eleanor's lap. She giggles. She is sparkling with joy.

I stand and watch them from a distance for a few moments before going over.

'You're not coming back, are you?' I say.

Eleanor shakes her head.

'These apes are barely apes any more. Someone has to teach them how to be wild again,' she says. 'They need me here.'

She picks up one of the babies, wraps it in a towel and cuddles it against her belly, resting the side of her face on the top of its head and rocking slightly. Deep down, I suspected she might stay. I *hoped* she would. I've always blamed myself for everything that happened here. This was my chance to make amends.

I stare at them, enjoying this sight for a few minutes, before noticing that Adhi has an expression of discomfort on his face. He is scratching the back of his head.

'I'm sorry, Ellie,' he says. 'But you cannot stay here.'

Eleanor looks up at him. She withers, loosening her grip on the chimp ever so slightly.

'What's the problem?' I say. 'You couldn't get a better orangutan expert anywhere in the world.'

'We don't need an expert. We don't want wild apes. They are good now. Everything works.'

Eleanor hides her face against the baby orang. None of us speaks. We look at the ground. And then, I see she is shaking slightly, sobbing. Despite all my intentions to make things right, I brought Eleanor back here after 20 years to break her heart all over again. She was right about me.

Caspar Stak, Black Window,
25th Anniversary Issue, August 2044.

The Captain

GREG HEARD THE beep of the dump truck's reverse alert and was instantly awake. He charged down the stairs, slammed open the many bolts on the door, and yelled 'Stop!' But his voice was lost in the sound of the truck's wheels crunching gravel and the hissing of its hydraulics.

The two men in the truck paid no notice to his shouting and arm waving when he burst out from his front door in his pants and t-shirt, walking in the way that one must on gravel in bare feet. The truck was as tall as his house and it was yellow. Already the dumper was inclining, the arms telescoping out, blotting out the low morning sun, and scaring off a gutter-full of house sparrows.

'Stop!' Greg called again. 'Not there you idiots!' He ran round the side of the truck, climbed up onto the driver's step and banged on the glass with the bottom of his fist. The man in the driver's seat turned his head to look at Greg in a bored way, raising his eyebrows. He pushed the red button on the dash.

Greg's expletives came out in an eloquent flurry, flecks of his spit spattering the glass. The tailgate dropped. The dumper continued its incline, until gravity broke the inertia of the bodies inside, and it spilled them in a great heap before Greg's front door.

Arms and legs wrestled against each other as they fell. Heads banged against heads and against his doorstep. Pale ankles bashed on bootscrapers.

'Not there!' Greg yelled one more time.

The truck's hydraulics chugged four times, repeatedly driving the dumper trailer up a few degrees, pushing out the remaining bodies, the ones that were stuck. These last few dived out, eyes still open, mouths agape, surprised refugees emerging into freedom after days in the dark.

Still in bed upstairs, Amanda wrapped her arms around her head, a soft helmet that covered her ears against her husband's shouting, his kicking of the front door. Cruelly, the clock showed just two minutes until it was time to get up. She did not feel that she'd slept at all, but she must have done, and with her mouth open, because her throat was sore, and her front teeth were dry and sticky. The minutes went quickly, and she felt she'd wasted them worrying through the list of things that needed to be packed for today's party.

In the kitchen, Greg had left the door flung open. Barely a sliver of sky and hedge was visible round the steep slope of corpses.

'Every damn time!' he said. 'The two minutes it would take them to open the gate and drive down into the field costs me a whole bloody day!'

Amanda shut the door against the smell from outside and moved around the kitchen like he wasn't there, pouring the last of the orange juice from the box into a cup, eating a piece of buttered toast which she'd folded in half for speed. There were three plastic crates on the dining room table, and into these she put boxes of eggs, bags of flour, cocoa and packs of butter, and then, as a protective layer over the top, three-dozen freshly washed children's aprons.

'I'm going to have to pay Wilkie and James to come help me again,' Greg continued. 'I'm going to call the council about it. I've had it this time.'

'Don't,' Amanda said. 'You'll make things much worse.'

'I'm losing money doing something they forced on me,'

he said. 'It's not...'

'Fair?' Amanda said. 'Show me one person who can say they're getting a fair deal.'

'I was going to say *efficient*,' he said. 'If their drivers were just two percent more helpful, I could have my day back.'

'At least they let us keep the place,' Amanda said. 'We have to be grateful for what we've got.'

'You always say that.'

'Other people are much worse off.'

'I have to call them. I have to. This is driving me crazy.'

'You've got more than yourself to think about now,' Amanda said, her fingers spread wide over her bulging stomach.

'Just two minutes,' Greg said. 'Two minutes and who knows, maybe I could actually *grow* something.'

Amanda put one crate on top of another and hefted it up on top of her stomach.

'Good god woman,' Greg said, 'put that down. Let me do it.'

'I'm going to have to do it myself at the hall,' she said.

'Get Melissa to help you.'

'Melissa is never on time.'

Greg took the two crates from Amanda and she picked up the remaining one. Together they side-stepped out of the door, round the heap, being careful not to tread on fingers, trying to ignore the faces.

A big black limousine with two little red flags mounted on its bonnet was parked up outside the town hall. Either side of the car were two military trucks. One of the many soldiers gathered around the trucks walked out into the road in front of Amanda's little Ford van and raised his hand.

Amanda wound down her window and smiled at the soldier. 'Good morning, sir,' she said. 'I'm here for Governor Franco-Basoni's party.' She inflected her voice at the end making it sound like a question.

The soldier called over one of his colleagues who was carrying a clipboard.

'Your name?' he said.

'Amanda Melman. From Cele-bake-tion.' She gestured to the side of the van, where the name of the company was printed.

'ID?'

'It hasn't arrived yet,' Amanda said. 'I have this problem every time. They misprinted my name. I sent it back three months ago. I'm just waiting for the new one. I keep chasing them.' Amanda took her bag from the passenger seat and pulled out a handful of envelopes. 'I have utility bills,' she said. 'And as you'll see, I've got cake-making stuff in the back. I'm not a terrorist, I promise.' Amanda made a big smile. It was not returned.

The soldier with the clipboard took the envelopes from her, opened up a couple and scanned through the bills. The other soldier walked around her truck, crouching down to examine the wheels, kneeling on the road to peer under the chassis.

'Okay,' the clipboard soldier said. He scored a line through her name on his sheet. 'Park around the back.'

'Thanks,' Amanda said. 'My friend who works with me will be arriving in a few minutes too. Her name's Melissa Hale. Just so you know.'

The soldier stared at her in a way that caused Amanda's cheeks to flush red. She wondered whether maybe she had breached some line of formality, and replayed what she'd said, in case there was an ambiguity that the soldier may have misinterpreted.

He waited the longest time before saying again, 'Park round the back.'

'Thank you,' she said. 'Have a lovely day.'

Her hand went to the window handle to close it, but she stopped and put her hands back on the steering wheel. The first soldier kicked her tyres as she drove away. She watched them watching her in her rear view mirror all the way to the car park.

Wilkie arrived with James in James's truck. The three men stood at the foot of the stinking mound of people, which was already attracting a noisy cloud of flies.

'Jeez,' Wilkie said. 'What a thing to wake up to.'

'You know what scares me?' Greg said. 'That one day this will become so normal I won't think about it.'

Wilkie put both hands flat on top of his head and gazed up the edifice of limbs. Many of the bodies were wearing suits. Smart shoes stuck out here and there, still laced. Women's bare feet with painted toenails. Wrists with watches that were still ticking. 'You should be more scared that you'll run out of land and they'll stop your subsidy,' Wilkie laughed. 'Then you'd really be screwed.'

'You can always dig deeper,' James said.

'Very profound,' Wilkie said. 'Come on Stephen Hawking, let's get this shifted before the sun gets hot.'

Melissa arrived in a cloud of perfume, clutching a stack of plastic boxes to her chest. Amanda was sweating in the heat, working fast to set out equal amounts of the cake ingredients on each of the nine tables.

'Where have you been?' Amanda said.

'The soldiers,' Melissa said. 'They wanted to search me before I came in. They were very thorough.'

'What *is* that perfume you're wearing?'

'I dropped the bottle in my lap in the car. I didn't have time to change.'

'Come on, they start arriving in half an hour.'

Four soldiers stood at the entrance to the hall, rifles on their backs, arms folded across their chests, watching Melissa and Amanda laying a stack of four aprons on each of the tables. Amanda patted down each stack to make it neat and flat. She put a wooden spoon into the mixing bowls, always at the eleven o'clock angle. Melissa opened up the plastic boxes and in individual ceramic bowls shared out crystallised fruits, Smarties, hundreds-and-thousands, and marshmallows.

One of the soldiers, a man with a big ginger beard, came and grabbed a handful of Smarties and clamped his hand over his mouth as he chucked them in. Melissa moved to replenish the bowl, but with a subtle move, no more than placing her fingertips on Melissa's forearm, Amanda stopped her. Together, the two women watched the man grin at them while he chewed. Amanda reciprocated his smile, but pulled it back when it encouraged the soldier's grin to widen enough to show a blue Smartie clamped between his teeth.

Greg reversed his truck close to the heap of bodies. Wilkie plucked an earring from the ear of a big dead woman at his feet. Her taupe skirt was torn all the way from her knee to her waist, and her enormous thigh spilled out, streaked with cellulite. Wilkie tossed the earring into a plastic washing up bowl on the doorstep.

James stood at her feet, bent forwards, hands on his knees, looking up and down her. He puffed out. 'How are we going to handle this one,' he said.

Wilkie grabbed her wrists. James grabbed her ankles. Wilkie said, 'One, two, three, lift.' They raised the woman from the ground. With her arms pulled taut above her head, her chin was forced forwards onto her chest, closing her mouth and rolling out a cushion of fat on which her frowning face rested.

'Lift man!' Wilkie said.

'I can't get a grip,' James said. The woman's wide ankles slipped through his fingers, and her bottom dropped to the ground.

'Your fingers are too small,' Wilkie said. 'They've still got some growing to do.'

'Up yours,' James said.

Greg jumped out of the cab, leaving the door open.

'Swap ends,' he said, and then to James, 'Take an armpit.'

Greg and James each hooked their forearms under the woman's armpits. Wilkie, the biggest of the three, grabbed her ankles and counted again. The three of them lifted her together.

Wilkie's face wrinkled with the effort, the bristles around his mouth rolling together into dark creases. The woman's ankles were slipping through his fingers. He hefted her up into the air a little, slid his grip up under her knees so he could lift her higher. The body sagged between them.

Wilkie began to count again, swinging her like he might a sack of potatoes. But James said, 'Don't. Not like that.'

'Oh give me a break,' Wilkie said. 'She's not going to feel it. I want to get home before dark.'

James looked to Greg.

'Let's just get her up before my back gives,' Greg said.

Wilkie began to count again, and this time, they swung together.

In the town hall kitchen, Amanda opened the oven and found it to be full of oily lumps of blackened crumbs and a shrivelled half-tomato. Melissa unpacked rubber gloves and fresh J-Cloths from her bag, filled a bowl with soap and hot water, and together they stuck their arms into the oven and began to scrub.

Kneeling like this, their heads close together, they filled the oven with whispers.

'I'm worried about Greg,' Amanda said. 'I'm worried he's going to do something stupid.'

'Like what?' Melissa said.

'I don't know. He gets crazier every morning when the truck arrives. He keeps talking about calling them up and complaining.'

'Well, what if he did?' Melissa said.

Amanda stopped to look at Melissa, frowning deeply.

'Are you serious?'

'He's got principles.'

'He can't afford to have principles,' Amanda said. 'He's going to be a dad. He's got more important things to think about.'

'I think I'd be proud of my husband if he stood up for himself.'

'You wouldn't say that if you had one.'

Melissa did not reply, but scraped a big blob of black foam from the back of her glove and flicked it into the bowl.

'I'm sorry,' Amanda said. 'I didn't mean that.' And then, 'Your perfume really is giving me a headache.'

The back of Greg's truck was filled, the peak of the bodies rising higher than the cab, held in place by weight and the interlocking of limbs. All three men heaved against the tailgate, pushing against the bodies, until the locking mechanism clicked into place. It had taken them an hour and a half to get a quarter of the heap onto the truck. Now the sun was higher and the flies more numerous. James went through the cleared space on the gravel, throwing stray shoes high up onto the truck. He picked up lost watches and coins from among the bloodied stones and threw them into the washing up bowl, which was now filling up.

'Can we have a cuppa before we set off?' James asked.

'We *should* pace ourselves,' Wilkie said.

'I want to get this done before it gets too hot,' Greg said. 'Let's stop for tea after we've unloaded this one.'

James wiped his hands on his jeans, and where he did, the denim was dark with dirt and other people's blood. Greg and Wilkie got in the cab.

'I'll ride on the outside,' James said, and he climbed up onto the driver's step, clinging to the mount of the wing mirror.

'You know I can't concentrate with your face peering in at me,' Greg said.

'Yeah,' Wilkie laughed. 'Why don't you just ride in the back.'

Greg set off down the track, his truck groaning and shuddering with every dip in the road. Thirst made the men quiet, and in this silence they could hear bodies slipping down the pile, things bumping into the painted steel sides, knuckles, shoes, foreheads, zippers, knees.

The children arrived dressed in various versions of the Captain outfits. Some of them had the official merchandise, produced in red polyester with foam padding to replicate his muscles on their scrawny chests. Others were home-made affairs, red t-shirts with a five-pointed star cut from yellow fabric and stitched on, the black fist at the centre of this logo drawn onto it with marker pens. Boys and girls wore the same costumes. As each new one arrived, they joined the dog-fight round the tables, chasing each other, both hands held out flat in front of them in the Captain's flying position. Every few seconds one would stop, spread his or her fingers, and then mimic with varying levels of success, the sound of the Captain's death ray, a sound most effectively rendered by screwing up the corner of the mouth, enough to twist the nose out of shape, biting the front teeth together and forcing out air in a slow, bubbly, hiss. Whereupon, the others would clutch their hearts and drop to the parquet floor, to lay for a few seconds before getting up and awaiting their turn to kill everyone.

'This is mental,' Melissa said. 'What's wrong with their parents?'

'Stop,' Amanda said. She tied a small knot in the strings of her apron at the zenith of her belly. Within a couple of weeks she would have to tie it round the back instead.

The birthday girl arrived, Sasha, her strut making her thick black hair swing from side to side behind her. Her mother, Governor Franco-Basoni, followed after, flanked by four soldiers. She looked around the room at each of the people present. When her gaze reached Amanda and Melissa, the two women nodded with respect. This gesture received nothing in return but an indifferent pout.

The soldier with the clipboard who had stopped Amanda earlier, came over and told the women that everyone had now arrived and they could begin.

A boy with his red face-paint already smudged around his mouth ran into the legs of the soldier, gripped the man's jacket and tugged at it with both hands. 'Is the Captain coming?' he said. 'When is the Captain coming?'

'You'll have to wait and see,' the soldier said, smiling for the first time and patting the boy's head.

The quarry was dug deep and wide, the road around it pummelled into chevrons by the tyres of earth-moving machinery. Gulls turned circles in the air above. Greg swung his truck round at the edge and James hopped off the driver's step to guide him back, getting the rear wheels as close to the edge as possible without danger of the ground crumbling away beneath them.

'You've still got some crops going then,' Wilkie said, pointing across the excavation to a field of tall stalks.

'Corn,' Greg said. 'Only about fifty hectares. But if I didn't grow *something* here, I'd go nuts.'

'Will it be edible?' James said, and when the other two gave him confused glares, he added, 'You know, with all this being right next to it.' James waved his hand around, gesturing at the pit.

'Give me a break,' Greg said.

Wilkie picked up a flint, pulled his arm all the way back and grunted as he threw it. The stone flew in a high arc, seeming to take forever to fall, and hit the ground with a soft thud, only a quarter of the way across the pit. Gulls and crows sprang up around the point of impact, complaining, and then settled back into their scavenging, amongst the flecks of pink, blue, white and grey where the clothes of the dead showed through the fine layer of dirt.

'This time last year,' Greg said, 'the government was paying me twice what they're paying now because I had skylarks nesting right here.'

'It won't always be like this,' James said. 'They'll find his weakness. Everyone has a weakness.'

'Who's they?' Wilkie said. '*They* think what they're doing now is the best thing for everyone. They're not even looking. This might be as good as it gets. Next year, we might look back to this moment and wish we still had the same freedoms we've got now.'

'Well that's a cheery thought,' Greg said. He unbolted the trailer's tailgate, and grabbed the trouser leg of a man already half falling out. 'Let's get this done.'

'What I was about to say,' Wilkie said. 'Is that *they* aren't going to do jack shit about it. It's down to us.'

While the cakes were baking, the kids watched a film. It was a montage of clips of the Captain set to a heavy-rock track. Some of the clips were high-quality, taken from news broadcasts. Others were jumpy and low-resolution, filmed on home movie cameras and mobile phones.

All of the town hall curtains were drawn. The kids sat on cushions on the floor, heads tilted back to watch the screen above them. They watched the Captain zipping past office blocks, thousands of windows shattering around him. They watched the Captain standing alongside generals at podiums, bathed in camera flashes. They watched the Captain land on a beach, raise his hands in his signature pose, the people in swimsuits leaping up terrified from their towels, feet kicking up sand as they ran to the water's edge to gather their children. And then everyone dropping, the whole beach felled in a second.

The children cheered.

'How can you stand this?' Melissa said, watching through the kitchen serving hatch. 'Would you let your kid sit through this?'

'Keep your voice down,' Amanda said.

'How can they watch this?'

'They don't understand,' Amanda said. She opened up the oven door and took out two trays of cakes and set them on the hob, before putting in the next two trays of mixture. Most of the cakes were lopsided mutants, spilling over the edge of their paper cups.

'This can't go on,' Melissa said.

Just then, Amanda noticed that the soldier with the ginger beard who'd eaten their Smarties earlier was stood outside the kitchen door, watching them both through the small square window.

Melissa wiped her hands on her apron. 'Would you like one?' she asked him, holding up a cake. 'Fresh out of the oven.'

The soldier wedged open the door with his boot and took the cake from her. He shoved the whole thing in his mouth in one go, severing it from the paper cup with his front teeth, watching Melissa the whole time.

'Good?' she said.

He nodded, chewing, and wiping crumbs from his beard. He looked around the kitchen, around the floor, behind the door, all around the work surfaces.

'Are you looking for something?' Melissa asked.

The soldier took another cake, then went back into the main hall, shutting the door behind him.

Amanda leaned up against the oven, puffing, shaking her head slowly at Melissa. Melissa came close, wiping up cake mixture with a cloth. 'Do you think he...' she began, but Amanda shook her head and pinched her lips together. 'You're going to get the wrong kind of attention wearing perfume like that,' she said.

The men were down to the last body, that of the big woman who was loaded onto the truck first back at the farmhouse. As before, Wilkie grabbed her ankles, James and Greg an armpit each. Wilkie didn't count this time, but they did swing, and couldn't help but watch the bulk of her, bouncing down the steeply chiselled quarry, her slow turns, hair streaming, the sudden acrobatic lunges when she connected with something jutting from the side, a rock, an irrigation pipe.

'What time is the party due to finish?' Wilkie asked.

Greg looked at his watch. 'In about half an hour.'

'So it could be happening now,' Wilkie said.

'Will she really do it?' James said. 'I mean...'

'Melissa's got bigger balls than the three of us put together,' Greg said.

'Yeah, but James is lowering our average,' Wilkie laughed.

James punched Wilkie's arm. 'This isn't the time,' James said. 'Jeez, I can't even think about it. I mean I can't stop thinking about it.'

Governor Franco-Basoni stood before all the children with the palms of her hands pressed together. 'I have a special treat for you,' she said.

The children all jumped up and down on the spot, their hands in the air, shouting, 'Captain! Captain!'

'Yes,' the Governor continued, 'especially for Sasha's birthday, because her family is so loyal, the Captain has come.'

Melissa and Amanda were wiping down the tables and repacking leftover ingredients into their plastic boxes. They watched the red-costumed man stride in through the front door. It was not the real Captain, but even a facsimile was enough to set Amanda's hands shaking.

The Captain raised his arms and all the children ran up to him, high-fiving him and calling out his name. 'And where is the birthday girl?' the Captain said. He was wearing a concealed voice changer, which gave his speech the unearthly metallic sound of the real Captain.

Governor Franco-Basoni looked across at Amanda, and mimed the action of lighting a candle with a match. Amanda nodded. The two women went into the kitchen and took out an enormous cake from its box. The red, yellow and black fondant icing on top was in the shape of the Captain's logo. Amanda's hands trembled as she stuck one candle into each of the five points of the star, and then three more gathered close together in the middle of the fist.

'You carry it,' Melissa said. 'I'll light the candles.'

Amanda agreed and handed Melissa the box of matches from her apron pocket. They waited at the kitchen door, just out of sight, for the signal.

The Captain began the first note of 'Happy Birthday', and everyone joined in. Melissa struck a match and lit a candle, then plucked it from the cake and used it to light the others before sticking it back in.

Governor Franco-Basoni bade them over with a flick of her hand. A soldier switched off the hall lights.

All the kids, the Governor and the Captain, turned to watch the cake approach, singing the happy birthday song together. Amanda forced a big grin. She could feel the heat of the candles on her face.

The children parted around Amanda and Melissa, so that they could get right up to Sasha, who was smiling broadly, the Captain's hand on her shoulder. Beside him, Governor Franco-Basoni clapped last and loudest at the end of the song.

In the middle of this applause, just as Sasha opened her mouth and sucked in a big breath of air in preparation for blowing out the candles, Melissa stuck her blouse sleeve into the tiny flames.

The substance she'd soaked her clothes with that morning ignited in one explosive whoosh. Everyone gathered around her was lit up by the flash, their terrified faces captured for a second as her blouse, trousers and hair ignited.

In the second that Melissa burst into flames, Amanda dropped the cake, the Captain stumbled back and tripped over his own heels, and the soldiers, suddenly awakened by duty, swung their guns round from their backs. It took a moment for the screaming to start, but already Melissa was charging at Governor Franco-Basoni, yelling out something, some kind of unintelligible valedictory cry.

So stunned was the Governor that she had taken only one step back when Melissa leaped at her, wrapped her arms and legs around her, and gripped tightly. They hit the ground, burning together.

Greg put the kettle on the Aga. Droplets of water rolled down its enamelled surface and fizzed and spat on the hot plate before disappearing in puffs of steam.

'Have you got any biscuits?' Wilkie said.

'There's some flapjack in there,' Greg said.

Wilkie took the square plastic box from on top of the microwave, opened up the corner and sniffed the air inside. James came back from the bathroom. His short fringe and the neck of his t-shirt were soaked where he'd wetted his face.

'Did Amanda know?' James said.

'No,' Greg said. He put out three mugs on the side and threw a teabag in each.

'Aren't you worried that...?'

'Amanda would never have let Melissa do it,' Wilkie said. 'She would have cancelled the whole gig. We would have missed the opportunity.'

'But what if they think Amanda was involved?'

'Give him a break,' Wilkie said. 'Yes Amanda's going to go ape shit, but that's what's going to convince them she's not involved. Her natural reaction will be the thing that gets her out of there.'

'You hope,' James said.

The kettle whistled. Greg poured water over the teabags, mashed them against the inside of the cups with the back of a teaspoon. 'Get the milk will you James,' he said.

'And will Amanda know that you knew?' James said. He opened the fridge, took out the bottle of milk, checked the use-by date on the side, and set it down on the work surface next to Greg. Greg grabbed his wrist, turned it over and squeezed with a force that caused James to gasp, to drop his shoulder, to grab at Greg's immoveable fist.

'Stoppit!' James said.

'Don't you dare question my morality,' Greg said. 'What have you ever risked? You weasel around with us, sitting at the back, piping up with your naïve observations when there's only one or two of us around. You think I'm not terrified? On the day you risk something, anything, you get to have an opinion, until then, just shut it.'

'Okay okay!' James said. 'I'm sorry!'

James rubbed at the red streaks Greg left on his wrist.

'*This* is great flapjack,' Wilkie said. His mouth was bulging with it. Greg poured milk into the tea, squeezed the teabags again, and tossed them in the compost pot. He carried the three mugs to the table. Wilkie raised his mug in a toast and said, 'Death to the Captain,' but before James or Greg could return the toast, the phone began to ring.

Amanda's hands were at her face, covered with icing, closing the horrified gape of her mouth. Children were screaming, soldiers pushing them out of the way, sending them skidding across the floor. The soldiers yelled at Melissa to let go of the Governor, their fear at the size and ferocity of the conflagration obvious in their hesitation. In response to Governor Franco-Basoni's screaming, and the thrashing of her legs, they kicked at Melissa, four of them, but Melissa's grip was strong. She was fused to the woman. The fire alarm began. The fake Captain scampered back on all fours to the edge of the hall, his voice changer amplifying his whimpers.

Only after someone had blasted the burning women with a foamy white jet from the fire extinguisher did the soldiers go at Melissa with their hands, peeling her apart from the Governor. There was smoke, and steam, and an acrid stench that made their eyes water. The soldiers yelled at her, spitting out curses, even though she was still.

Amanda was paralysed by all of this, standing in the same spot she'd been when Sasha was about to blow out the candles, the cake broken over her feet, but then the soldiers began thudding Melissa with the butts of their rifles, and Amanda became galvanised.

'Stop!' she yelled. 'It was an accident!'

She took one step towards her fallen friend when a soldier tackled her from the side, his shoulder hitting her thigh with awful force. Her feet skittered in the air for purchase as she fell, crying out, 'I'm pregnant.' The soldier crashed on top of her, crushing her. His elbows pinned her arms. A big metallic-tasting palm covered her mouth, pushed her head to the side. And then there were more around her, pointing their rifles in her face, telling her not to move.

Greg got up from the table and lifted the handset from its cradle. The number calling was unknown. His thumb was on the answer button, but he didn't press it yet. Each ring startled the whole kitchen.

He was at the open door. The heap of bodies only slightly diminished. Now the crows and the magpies had found it, hopping from limb to limb, blinking and squabbling.

There were only two rings left before the answerphone would cut in. Greg was shaking. Had Melissa succeeded? Had they gone too far? Had the world changed? Had it changed enough to make the sacrifice worth it? Could he live with the consequences?

Under the weight of all the possibilities, Greg pushed the button and took the call.

A Thousand Seams

MOLLY WAS KNEADING the school uniforms in the sink when she noticed the blood spots. There were four of them, of different sizes, along the right shoulder of the shirt. In the candlelight they were almost black, and they faded only slightly in the foamy water under the attentions of her thumbs. She took the dishcloth from the oven handle and worked her fingers dry on the way to the living room.

Her sons, Ben and Raf, lay on opposite ends of the sofa under a patchwork quilt that Molly had made from their old babygros. Ben was reading a Superman comic with a torch. Raf, the younger of the two, was already asleep.

'Ben?' Molly said. 'Did something happen today? Are you injured, pumpkin?'

'No,' he said, but even in the dim candlelight the lie was plain on his face.

'Let me see,' she said, taking the torch from him.

'Hey! I was reading.'

Ben squirmed from her touch and covered his shoulder with his hands, but Molly was indomitable.

The neck of his jersey pyjamas slipped easily over his shoulder, stretched as it was from his chewing. Molly explored his bare shoulder in the circle of torchlight, the tip of her nose almost brushing against him.

'Stop breathing on me,' he said.

'Shush now.'

Molly could see nothing, and at first was relieved. Maybe it hadn't been blood on his shirt after all. But then

Ben's movements as he tried to wriggle free from her caused the mouth of the wound to gape a little. The split was an inch long.

'Stop your fidgeting,' she said. 'You'll make it worse. Why'd you not tell me you were hurt? You have to tell me straightaway. Why didn't the school call me? Did your teacher know? How did it happen? Who did this?'

'It was no one. It just happened.'

'Don't move. I'll get the kit.'

'No!' he said.

'Don't be daft now.'

The kit was kept in a red biscuit assortment box in the Welsh dresser. Even in the dark, Molly's hands knew where to find it. Back at the sofa, she gave Ben a candle on a saucer by which to read his comic. 'Keep your hair away from it,' she said. Then she woke up Raf.

'I'm asleep!' he complained. She put the torch in his hands.

'I know squish, but Ben's tired too, and he can't go to sleep till he's fixed up.'

'Why do *I* always have to help?'

'Don't be a bugger now,' she said. 'How do I ask the first time I ask?'

'Nicely,' Raf said, slipping his feet out from under the blanket. He stumbled, eyes barely open, round the back of the sofa to the other side, where Molly put the torch in his hands and moved it into position above Ben's shoulder.

'Sorry sweet chucks,' she said. 'You'll both be tucked up in bed in just a minute. Now don't move.'

'I can still go to the Lights, can't I?' Ben said.

'*If* you keep yourself safe. No roughhousing, okay?'

'Okay.'

Molly popped open the red kit box and took out three butterfly plasters. She put one foot up on the arm of the sofa, readjusted her long skirt, then lined the plasters up along the top of her thigh. She told both boys to keep very still once more, and then she began.

Molly heard Chris's keys in the lock as she was tucking Ben into bed. He called out hello, but she didn't shout back, as Raf was already asleep on the top bunk, and Ben was almost gone too. With him so dozy, his fingers didn't want to go into the gloves, so Molly had to take them off again, rest his hand on her knee, and try to line up his fingers and thumb with the fingers and thumb of the glove.

'Hello!' Chris called again. 'I'm home!' He was on the stairs now, but still too far for Molly to shout. Instead, she picked up one of Ben's arm braces and peeled apart a Velcro strap. The sound guided Chris to her in just a few seconds.

He brought with him the smell of outside, of chimney smoke and garbage. 'You've left the candles going downstairs,' he said. He put his hand on top of her head and lightly squished her toes with the ball of his foot. They were both wearing two pairs of socks each, and to Molly the soft pressure of his foot felt good. 'Do that again,' she said.

'I don't want you to burn the house down while I'm out,' he said.

'I don't like it when it's dark. Have you eaten?'

'No. And I worked through lunch.'

'Is there any news?'

'Not yet, but it'll be this week. They've been holed up in the meeting room all day. We've been trying to earwig but didn't get anything. I feel sick. I feel physically sick.'

'Do you not want your dinner then?'

'I can still eat.'

'It's on the hob. I ate with the boys.'

Chris put his foot on the frame of the bunk bed and climbed up to kiss Raf. Then he squatted down, moved Ben's fringe aside and kissed his forehead.

Ben opened his eyes. 'Can I just have the gloves on tonight?' he said.

'Don't Ben, please,' Molly said. She pulled all four Velcro straps open, and as she did the last one, the electricity came back on. The boiler fired up with a whooshing sound. From all around the house, came ticking, humming and bubbling noises as the television, the radio, the heating, and a dozen other devices pinged back into life.

At the school, Molly wished she'd caught Miss Prentice just a few minutes earlier. Ben's teacher was heading out of the staff room to her class, and now that Molly had her attention, she had to say her piece, even though she'd not nearly enough time to get into it the way she wanted to get into it. Molly couldn't bear to come back later. She'd spent all morning preparing herself and didn't want to go off the boil.

'I only have a moment,' Miss Prentice said.

'Ben came home with an injury yesterday,' Molly said. She slipped one foot from its flat shoe and rubbed the arch against her calf.

'As far as I'm–'

'You know we can't afford for him to be having accidents.'

'Yes, we–'

'I know you have a lot of kids to look after, but you've none that are fragile like Ben, have you?'

Miss Prentice, a slight thing, made Molly feel like a brawny beast, made her arms folded across her chest feel beefy, her feet like great big hooves.

'Of course we recognise that,' Miss Prentice said. 'He's never in a situation where there isn't an adult present.'

'So how did it happen then? And what did happen? Ben won't say a word. You know how he can be.'

Miss Prentice nodded. 'I wasn't there at the time, one of our teaching assistants was, but I gather there was a small argument at lunchtime. They were playing a bit rough. The school nurse checked him over straight after, but didn't see any injuries. That's why we didn't mention anything.'

'Well he did have an injury.'

'I'm not sure there's anything else we could have done.

The fight was broken up as soon as it began. Look, I'm very sorry but I have to get to class now.'

'Ben's not the fighting kind,' Molly said. 'He knows better. I have to be certain that someone's keeping watch over him the whole time, putting a lid on any nonsense before it happens. I have to be able to trust that he'll be safe while he's in your care. I can't be here to watch over him, you've already made that quite clear.'

'We obviously can't provide one-on-one supervision for him throughout the day,' Miss Prentice said, moving away now. Molly followed to maintain the distance between them. 'There's a limit to what we can do, but we do as much as we can. Again, it might be that you need to look at other options.'

'He's not switching schools. He goes through enough. There's an absolute bare minimum of care that Ben needs, and you have to provide it. I need you to promise me that you'll do enough. I need you to reassure me.'

'I can't promise you that this will never happen again. Boys bicker.'

'Ben can't afford to bicker. And what of the other boy, the one that hurt him? What's happened about him?'

'What's happened?'

'What kind of discipline did he get?'

'Mrs Glock,' the teacher said, looking confused, 'he was fighting with his brother.'

Raf worked his face red and his pillow wet, so insistent was he that he'd done nothing wrong. Regardless of the neighbours, Molly poured out her wrath with such force that her throat was raw before she was done. She spared him nothing.

And when they were both spent, Molly sat Raf up, curled him into the shell of her arm, and wiped his wet face with her sleeve. 'You could have killed him,' she said. 'How many times must I tell you? You're his brother for God's sake.

You're supposed to be the one to protect him. He can't play rough like you can.'

'But he's older than me!'

'I know you didn't mean to hurt him, but what if you went too far?'

Announced by his heavy footsteps on the stairs, Chris arrived at the boys' bedroom door. 'What's happened now?' he said. As Molly explained, more to Raf to reinforce the message than to her husband, Chris wiggled his lower jaw between thumb and forefinger, as if this news had somehow nudged it from its hinges. He had nothing to say on the matter and just stood there, mesmerized by the closed curtains, snatching back the breaths that the stairs had taken from him.

'Any news?' Molly asked.

'Nothing.'

'We have to talk later. When we've all had dinner.'

'About?'

'Mr Belgrave called.'

'Oh.'

All of Molly's boys, Ben, Raf and Chris, ate with an eager carelessness that caused the prongs of their forks to clack against their teeth. It made Molly shudder to watch the way Ben stuffed each forkful through his lips.

At birth that mouth could not close, but now Ben could narrow it to the circumference of a single strand of spaghetti. It was a pleasure to watch tomato sauce, stripped from the pasta, gather on his lips to be harvested by his tongue.

When Ben was born, his upper lip had been cleft in two places. The lip was composed of three parts, the splits between them running right through the gum, and all the way up into his nostrils, flattening his nose and making of his mouth a complicated flower, which Molly had struggled to feed with her nipple. The nurses had advised that bottle-feeding might be more effective, but Molly was determined. 'If he learns the bottle, he'll never get back on the breast,' she said. This belief grew out of a general philosophy about life, a philosophy she had inherited from her grandfather, the hardest working person she had ever known. Molly's grandfather had taught her, through example not instruction, that every choice she made for the sake of comfort and ease would cause her to become weaker, less resilient, less able to deal with the next situation life threw at her.

He'd never summarized this philosophy into a neat motto. This was something Molly had always wanted to do. The closest she'd come so far was: 'If you choose easy today, then like it or not, you'll get difficult tomorrow'. It wasn't quite right. She knew this. She lived the principle faithfully, even if she hadn't yet reduced it into the kind of saying that people could carry about in their mouths, a saying easily remembered because it contains rhyme or alliteration. Her ambition, aside from raising her boys to be strong, independent men, was to contribute to the world a new motto, the one that had so benefited her and her grandfather's lives – their family philosophy of strength through the deliberate choice of difficulty.

There was a sunken place on the left side of the sofa where a spring had gone, and when Molly and Chris cuddled here with their cups of tea, the depression pushed their bottoms together in a way that Molly found most comforting. Chris smelled of hard work, but he was warm, and even though a power cut had snuffed out the electricity in the middle of the boys' bedtime routine, there was no meat in the freezer to go off, and they had a fat candle on the table, which was ripe for gazing.

'So what did he say then?' Chris said.

Molly shifted to the other side of the sofa so she could face him. She put her legs in his lap. 'Hold my feet would you,' she said.

While Molly related the call from Mr Belgrave, her ear grew hot with the memory of the conversation. The line had been terrible, and she'd had to press the phone hard against her ear to make out what was said.

'He's done the operation three times before,' Molly said.

'Well that's good.'

'Twice it was successful, but one time... not.'

'What happened to the kid?'

Molly shook her head. Chris sipped his tea.

'Well, is it as straightforward as that, a one in three chance?' Chris said. 'Were the situations the same in every case? Were they the same as Ben's?'

'I don't know.'

'Well what did he tell you?'

'He said so much.'

With Chris behaving like this, the facts had muddled in her memory. What had Mr Belgrave talked about all that time? There was not an hour's worth of information in her head.

'So what's your feeling about it?' Chris said.

'I don't know. This isn't just my decision.'

'You're not giving me enough facts to make a decision. I need to know everything. I need specifics.'

'Don't be like that.'

'I'm not. But you're asking me to make a big choice about our son's life and all you're basically telling me is that there's a one in three chance it could go pear-shaped.'

'Pear-shaped?' Molly withdrew her feet and fled the room, refusing to even hear his apologies. Upstairs she waited on the edge of the bed. It was cold. When she listened hard, she heard the base of his mug set down upon the table.

Chris broke open the barrel containing his home brew earlier than he'd planned because Holby and Gert had come round. Today Holby had been one of the first five at the plant to lose their jobs. This was the first beer Chris had ever brewed, and though it was flat and yeasty, helped down with salted peanuts it did soften the edges of the evening somewhat. Molly smiled, by way of encouragement, as she sipped the brown froth from the edges and said that it was good.

Their conversation could not be diverted from Holby's redundancy and the threat of another 12 to be made at the plant in the next week. When Gert's sobbing was bringing out the silence in all of them, Molly took her into the kitchen and set the kettle on the stove.

'I know I've got no right to be complaining to you,' Gert said. 'When you've been through so much, but I just don't know what we're going to do.'

Molly felt bad that she had no tissue to offer Gert, that she had to watch the woman dab at her nose with her cardigan sleeve.

'These things are only revealed to us as fast as we can cope with them,' Molly said. 'You wait, in six months this will all be a distant memory.'

In the living room, Holby and Chris were whispering and shaking fresh peanuts into the bowl.

'I honestly don't know how you do it,' Gert said.

'You need to make a plan,' Molly said. 'Something to look forward to.'

'Is that how you cope?'

'I don't like to talk about me,' Molly said. But Gert wouldn't let up. Molly said she had to check on the boys. She hid up in their room with her eyes closed, enjoying the warmth of Ben's back against her palm. It calmed her to feel each breath inflate his body.

But then there were footsteps on the stairs, and a moment later, Gert's face poking into the room. 'Knock knock,' she whispered. Before Molly could even think about getting up, Gert was there, crouched at her feet, patting Molly's leg and making that awful sympathetic face of hers.

'I really don't want to talk about it,' Molly said when Gert asked how Ben was doing. But Gert was relentless with the questions and Molly couldn't help but give up just a little, tiny details that the woman set upon hungrily.

'You poor things,' Gert said. Her hand stayed on Molly's knee and Molly was powerless to move it even though it made her shiver all over.

'You get on with life,' Molly said. 'You have to. There are people worse off.'

'It's just so unfair,' Gert whispered. She stood up and sat beside Molly on Ben's bed, putting her arm around her and squeezing her shoulder in a side-on hug, an invasion which made a plank of Molly's body.

Morning. Molly ran upstairs to the bathroom with a kettle and told Raf to keep his feet back as she poured the boiling water at the plug end of the bath.

'Why do I have to have a bath with him?' Raf said.

'Because together your little bums displace more water so you get a deeper bath,' she said. 'Now get to work with that flannel.'

From the hallway, Chris called up with his goodbyes.

'Make sure you're home on time tonight, love,' she said. 'We don't want to be late for the Lights, do we boys?'

The front door opened to the sound of a bicycle going past, and then Chris was gone for the day. Molly rolled up her sleeves and dunked Ben's soft yellow sponge in the water. Her dabs upon the patchwork of his skin were slow and gentle, and when she was done, she was giddy from holding her breath.

Later, with the house to herself, Molly toasted and buttered a crumpet. She sat on the sofa to eat it, next to the pile of Ben and Raf's school trousers that needed the knees stitching up. She was chewing the first mouthful when the electricity clicked off. She spat the mouthful on the plate, took the plate to the kitchen, and scraped it into the bin. She put on her boots and duffel coat and fled the house with no plans but to walk.

Night. It took Molly much bellowing to get Raf and Ben's feet into wellingtons. Outside their open door, puddles were already gathering in the pot holes.

'Are we really taking them out in this?' Chris said.

'Look at their little faces,' Molly said, cupping a palm over Ben's cheek. 'Would you have them disappointed?'

Their open door turned the heads of each of the people walking past, their nosy faces caught for an embarrassed moment in the glow of the Glocks' bare hallway bulb.

'Well let's either get out or close the door,' Chris said.

Outside, the crowd thickened as the streets narrowed. The rumbling of so many boots chased mallards from their roosts. Chris carried a golfing umbrella big enough for all four of them. He held it high because Molly kept telling him to keep it away from people's eyes. The Glocks' umbrella came together with other umbrellas, forming a river of taut nylon triangles that slowed as it approached the quayside.

In the market square, the air smelled of sweet batter hitting buttered hotplates. A row of iron braziers cast flickering shadows onto St Mary's. Silhouettes of men with flat-caps and turned-up collars stuffed table legs and two-by-fours into the braziers, throwing out bright sparks that meandered over the crowd until the raindrops snuffed them out.

There were also men and women with placards protesting about the state of things, the power cuts and the redundancies. They moved in a long caterpillar through the crowd, chanting 'Cut your bonuses, not our throats.'

'Couldn't they have left it for tonight?' Molly said.

'I should be with them,' Chris said.

'You should be with us.'

The Lights had always been Molly's favourite night of the year. Just thinking about watching the candle parade from the perch of her grandfather's shoulders caused a rush of nostalgia so intoxicating that no worries could stand against it. She'd been to almost every parade since her birth, even asleep in a sling across her mother's chest. Whatever might happen in between parades, eventually there would always be the Lights, the smell of the crêpe stalls and the spit roasts, and the sweet hymns that went right through her.

The best position was along the sea wall overlooking the breakwater, where the parade would end. From here, you could see the choir coming all the way down the hill, disappear into the cobbled maze of the town, then emerge at the mouth of the market square. Chris took Raf to join the long queue for pancakes. Molly headed for her spot. She steered through the crowd with the prow of her shoulder, keeping Ben in her lee.

Chris and Raf got back with the pancakes just in time, and the boys set to covering their faces with chocolate. The rain had let up enough for people to collapse their umbrellas. Already, the singers were moving along the breakwater. 'Look at their reflections in the sea,' Molly said. Something about all that candlelight, jostling on the surface of the waves, stirred up warmth in her belly.

Molly leaned back against Chris, took his arms and wrapped them around herself. She rested her cheek on his sleeve. Though the wool of his jacket was scratchy, there was comfort in it still.

Molly had only ever missed one candle parade. The one just after Ben was born, before his first operation, when other people had given her son looks that all but broke her, when she couldn't bear to be out.

Mr Belgrave had reassured her then that the human body has a thousand seams, and that just one of Ben's was undone. Operating on him was just a case of stitching it up and then he'd be complete. It had been a comfort to think that it was such a small part.

This was before anyone had realised that not one, but every one of Ben's seams was weak, news they didn't think they could ever swallow.

Thanks to her grandfather's philosophy, Molly had always approached hard decisions about her own life with a kind of gratitude, because choosing the hard path made her better, more independent, gave her an advantage over those that chose comfort. But whatever armour years of adhering to this philosophy had given her, it became redundant when Ben was born, when the most tender inner part of herself had been brought to the outside, vulnerable to the worst of the world.

Before Ben, Molly would willingly submit herself to any difficulty, accepting that however it pained her, she would gain strength from it. But she could never submit Ben to the same. Making hard decisions about her child's life involved a responsibility unimaginable before she had become a parent. And the decision was definitely hers to make. Chris would not speak first. He would only agree or disagree with her. This was his way.

Molly longed for the sense of safety she'd felt watching the Lights on the breakwater from her grandfather's shoulders. For just a moment, thinking about him and watching the Lights, she almost had the phrase that had eluded him. That encapsulated her inherited beliefs. But as the singing came across the water, and she tangled her fingers in Ben and Raf's hair, there came another noise from behind and the words fell from her.

All around, people turned away from the Lights to look back in the direction of St Mary's, where the caterpillar of protesters was coming apart, their placards pitching left and right and dropping down into the crowd. There were shouts. Blue lights from two police cars flashed against the shop fronts.

Even though the tumult was happening a way off, its ripples spread all the way through the crowd to Molly and the boys on the sea wall. Molly felt herself pushed against the metal railing, its hard edge digging into her side.

'We have to get out,' Molly said.

'But the fireworks haven't started yet!' Raf said.

'What's the problem?' Chris asked.

'Just move, now.'

'It's nothing.'

Though Ben was heavy, she picked him up and bore his complaining in her ear. 'Right now,' she said.

Chris looked at her for a moment, then, rolling his eyes and shaking his head, he picked up Raf and began sidestepping through the crowd, a little at a time, towards the quiet pedestrian streets that began by the breakwater, where the choir, unaware of the commotion, sung on. Molly pushed at Chris's back with her elbow. 'Move quicker,' she said, holding Ben tight against her, wincing with every knock he took. She stepped on someone's toe and they complained 'Hey!', their hand coming to her shoulder.

'Don't you touch me,' she said, and then, becoming aware of her teeth, she closed her mouth and pushed on.

Behind them, the shouts grew louder, more frequent, forcing Molly's footsteps onto Chris's heels. She grew breathless. Ben was a weight. Would it always be like this for him, she wondered. Fleeing every fight, however small, because his body could not hold its integrity in a struggle. Ben's condition deprived him of the thing she prized most in herself – the ability to be strengthened by difficulty. Without that, could he ever feel satisfied or whole? Could he ever be independent? What would happen when she was old, or sick or dead? What then? Would his brother have to take the responsibility? Would he even do that? Or would he run away, as far and as fast and as soon as he could?

The crowd tightened around them, jostling as the protest polarised people to move towards or away from it. A woman's hand struck Ben's arm as she tried to push her way past and he yelped. Molly kicked at the woman, caught her calf, made her cry out and fall forward onto her knees. Molly pushed past her, panting now, so hot in her coat.

'It's okay baby,' she said into Ben's ear. 'I'm going to get us out of here. I'm going to make everything okay.'

The Stormchasers

IT'S SO WINDY today. My son Jakey and I are at the window watching leylandii trees bow to each other, and the snails being blown across the patio like sailboats.

We've been watching for 15 minutes or so when Jakey says, 'I'm scared.'

'Of what?' I ask.

'Of tornadoes.'

'Listen,' I say, 'no tornadoes are coming here. Even if we got in the car right now and drove around all day like the stormchasers on TV, we'd be lucky to find one. Very lucky.'

'But what if we did?'

There is a noise from behind us. We both look at the fireplace. The wind is playing the chimney like a flute.

'Even if we were really lucky and did find one,' I say, 'in England it would be a tiny thing. We don't get the big ones here.'

'An F4?' he asks. We have watched documentaries about tornadoes together since he was a baby. Among six-year-olds, he is an expert.

'No way,' I say. 'An F2, if we were *really* lucky.'

'Big enough to suck up a person?'

He is imagining the tornado like a straw in the sky's mouth, I can see this.

'Nuh-uh,' I say. 'Just big enough to fling a couple of roof tiles about, or knock over some flowerpots, or break a greenhouse to pieces.'

'But what if...' he starts.

He is not going to believe me, sitting here in the house with the wind whoo-whooing around our walls like a ghost.

'Go get changed out of your jim-jams,' I say. 'I'll show you that there's nothing to be afraid of.'

While Jakey looks for his shoes, I pack lunch for us in a cotton shoulder bag: for me, chicken-liver pâté and apple chutney sandwiches, and a flask of Earl Grey tea; for Jakey, cheese spread sandwiches, a fun-size Twix and two cartons of apple juice.

'All set?' I say when he gets to the bottom of the stairs. He is wearing the bright yellow sou'wester and macintosh that he has finally grown into. I bought them for him before he was born, when he was just in my imagination.

'Uh-huh,' he says.

'We'd better go say goodbye to Mum,' I say.

We creep upstairs together, peep around the bedroom door. Mum is still in bed. She has the light out. Yesterday the dentist at the hospital pulled four wisdom teeth from her mouth. She has been in bed for a whole day, and mostly silent.

'Where are you going?' she says. Even her voice sounds wounded.

'We're going tornado chasing,' Jakey says.

'We won't be long,' I say. 'Can I get you anything?'

'No.'

'Are you feeling okay?' Jakey asks.

She pulls the duvet over her head. 'Just go away,' she says.

We drive.

'It feels good to be out, doesn't it?' I say. 'Seen any tornadoes yet?'

Jakey looks around. He says nothing.

The bendy roads between the hedgerows are full of fallen branches so I go slow. We live in the countryside, a little house all on its own. In the summer, from the air, our plot is a dark green triangle in the middle of a bright yellow sea of rapeseed. I have seen it from the air, in a microlight. The photograph I took is in our bathroom. I stare at it every time I pee.

'Where shall we go?' I say. 'If we were proper stormchasers, Jakey, we'd have a Doppler radar and a laptop so we could find the tornadic part of the storm.'

'We *are* real stormchasers,' he says.

I'm watching the road carefully but I can see his pout from the corner of my eye.

'You're right,' I say. 'But we don't have Doppler, so we'll have to rely on our instincts. You take a look at the sky and tell me where you think the tornadoes will touch down.'

Jakey presses the window button till the window is open the whole way. He sticks his head out. I slow the car and move into the middle of the road so he doesn't get hit by the sticky-out branches that the hedge-mower has missed. I'm going slow enough that I can watch Jakey. He is looking up into the sky, holding the door frame with both hands. The wind is throwing his shaggy hair all around his head. His hair is cornfield-blond, the same as mine. His mum's is almost black. 'Yet another thing he got from you, not me,' she sometimes says.

'That way,' he says, pointing north-east.

When we get to the motorway, the car is hard to control. The wind bullies our left hand side. The windscreen wipers are overwhelmed with this much rain. We feel enclosed, in the car. We are like a head in a hood. Jakey gets to choose the radio station. He chooses pop music. He sings along.

'How do you know the words to all these songs?' I ask.

'Mum listens to this radio station,' he says.

I do not like pop music, but I do like to hear Jakey sing.

We've been driving for 20 minutes, when ahead we see a smudge of yellow on the horizon. The rain is thinning. The cars coming towards us on the other side of the motorway have their lights off. In the rear-view mirror is a procession of lit headlamps, bright against the bruise-black sky.

'We should turn around,' I say.

'No. It's this way,' Jakey says.

'Are you sure?'

'Uh-huh.'

We reach sunlight. The wet tarmac around us is steaming.

'Are you sure the tornadoes are this way Jakey?'

'No.'

'Shall we turn around?'

It looks like the end of the world back the way we came. Within the wall of cloud, there's a heck of a light show.

'Okay,' Jakey says.

I come off the motorway and go round the roundabout three times – our game when Mum's not in the car. Jakey giggles, pinned to the door by physics.

We go back the way we came. I break the speed limit now because the storm is running away from us. We eat our lunches from our laps while we drive.

'If you're scared of tornadoes,' I say, 'why do you want to see one so badly?'

Jakey shrugs, finishing his apple juice. It gurgles at the bottom of the carton.

'Well, I told you we'd be very lucky to see one. Stormchasers drive thousands of miles to find them, drive around for weeks sometimes.'

'How far have we driven?'

'About 80 miles. Shall we go home now? Mum'll be wondering where we are.'

'Yes,' he says.

The sun follows us back. We lead it all the way to our front gates. Jakey picks up handfuls of the leaves that are heaped against our porch and drops them again. I put Jakey's lunch rubbish in the cotton bag before I get out. I open the front door and we both go inside.

'We're home!' I call, wiping my feet.

No answer.

I tiptoe upstairs. Our bed is empty.

'Dad!' Jakey calls out.

I run downstairs.

In the living room, the coffee table is on its side against the wall. One of its legs is broken off. The TV is face down on the carpet. The mantelpiece above the fireplace is bare. All the photos and pinecones and holiday souvenirs are on the floor. Some are smashed on the slate tiles in front of the wood burner. On the walls, the pictures are all at angles. Jakey's toys are tipped from his box.

In the middle of it all, sitting on the floor with her arms round her legs, and her forehead on her knees, is Mummy. Her knuckles are bloody.

Jakey moves towards her. I hold him back with my hand.

'Don't. There's glass,' I say. 'You okay Mummy? Did you see it, the tornado? When it came through?'

No answer. No movement.

Only she and I know that the story about the dentist was a terrible lie.

Santa Carla Day

THE YOUNG SHARKS were laid out in enormous paddling pools on the boardwalk. Three of them. Each with a rubber hose stuck in the corner of its mouth. Their exposed backs and dorsal fins grew dull in the sunshine. Finch crouched beside the largest of them, the tiger shark, longer than he was tall, and with a brutal girth. Stripes decorated its upper-side like sunlight on the ocean floor. Finch's bent knee leaned into and buckled the edge of the pool, causing saltwater to spill out across the hot boards. He pushed a thick needle into the shark's side, topping up the anaesthetic. Really this should have been done within the cool darkness of the aquarium, but even these preparations were part of the Santa Carla Day show. It was important to build anticipation.

On the low walls around the lagoon beside the Tolebaro Aquarium, there were folks in their sandals, licking ice cream from their knuckles, taking photos. Finch made sure that as he worked on each of the sharks, he positioned himself so that the spectators would not go home with pictures of his back, but would see the full intensity of his concentration, the strength of his grip on the pliers, the sharks' mouths pulled open, and inside, the crystal garden of teeth, bone-bright in the sun.

A small rowing boat, overburdened with boys and deep in the water, pulled up to the steps. Seawater sloshed in as they rocked it this way and that, singing some fraternal shanty and goading one of their number to climb out onto the dock.

Giving in to their jeers and their slaps at his back, the young boy plucked his hands from his baggy pockets and held them up in the air, cheerfully defeated. He ran up the steps towards Finch, his flip-flops making a fine slapping sound that shot the whole way across Tolebaro Bay.

The boy came close, hands on his hips, his shadow a bold arrow cast down at Finch's feet.

'Hector,' Finch gave a little upwards nod. 'Come for a look?'

'I thought they'd be bigger,' Hector said, stroking his dark fringe back from his eyes.

'Really?' Finch laughed. 'Well, they'll look a lot bigger in the water, when they're moving. This is the one to watch out for.'

Hector crouched down with Finch beside the mean wedge of the tiger shark's head. Water from the hose spilled out through its gills.

'This is a female,' Finch said. 'Just a year old. Next summer she'll be twice as long again.' Finch pulled the snout back. 'See how the teeth flex forward like that?' he said. 'Whenever a tooth gets knocked out, another one swivels in to take its place.'

Hector reached out to touch the serrated front edge of a tooth, but hesitated.

'It's okay,' Finch said. 'She won't wake up. See how the teeth are shaped like a can opener? There's a part for puncturing and a part for sawing. Out in the ocean they eat big old turtles. They go through those tough shells like a spoon through the top of a crème brûlée.'

At the moment that Hector touched fingertip to tooth, someone behind him, one of his friends, screamed loudly, and the other four all laughed, bounding up the steps, full of vim.

'If you want to help, boys,' Finch said. 'You can fill those buckets and pour water over their backs.'

They looked at each other for a moment, and then,

giggling, squabbled over the buckets, of which there were only four between five. Something about being entrusted with this responsibility sobered the boys. They emptied the buckets over the length of the two bull sharks with gentle reverence, taking special care over the sharks' faces, their unclosing eyes, and their cruel mouths, which dribbled fresh blood when disturbed.

'It feels rough,' Hector said, his hand now on the tiger shark's head.

'Rough enough to take your skin off,' Finch said. 'Tigers circle you, bump you, slap you with their tails. They move slow, then zip in, lightning fast. That tall dorsal fin helps them turn tight circles. They come at you in quick blasts. Sometimes they're so fast, you don't know you've been bit till they're way off already. And then when you think they're gone, you see the fin swivel in the water and they come back.'

'Where's the best place to hit them with the paddle?'

Finch laughed. 'On the day, you'll be so scared you won't have the mind to find a target and hit it.'

'I'm not scared.'

'No? Well, in that case, when you strike, the only vulnerable areas are the eyes and the gills. Give 'em a good enough whack and they'll leave you alone. But is that what you want?'

'How do you mean?'

'Well, the whole town will be watching you. You've been chosen over every other kid in Tolebaro. You've got to give them a good show. How you perform will set how they all see you for the rest of your life. Do you want to be the boy who hit the sharks accurately, bop bop bop, and scared them all away, only to stand there looking like a idiot for the remainder of the 71 seconds, or do you want to be the boy who had the epic battle, who, when the sharks went at him, took it like a man?'

Hector stared at the sunlight flashing on the surface of the water.

'They can't hurt you, anyway,' Finch said. 'Not really. However bad they attack, you'll walk out of there, red and sore of course, but with just a few bruises. But that's what you want isn't it? When you walk out of that pool, you want to look like you've survived an ordeal. You want everyone to look at you and think: "I would never have the balls to do that." On Santa Carla Day, you'll be the king of the town. Better to look like you earned it, don't you think?'

Hector smiled.

Finch widened the mouth of the shark, propping its snout up with his elbow, the heel of his hand on the lower jaw. A hundred teeth fanned forwards and Hector backed away from the smell. Finch clamped one of the big front teeth with his pliers, and with a practised curl of his wrist, plucked it and dropped it onto the boards.

'Can I keep that?' Hector said, picking up the tooth and wiping the blood from it with his thumb.

'Sure,' Finch said. 'You can have a whole bucket full if you like, once I've got the rest out.' He set the pliers to the next tooth and pulled.

Finch came home to the sound of thumping upstairs. His wife, Nina, was at the sink, scouring limescale from the bottom of a big glass vase. The radio was turned up way too loud.

'What's going on?' he asked.

'I told him he had to pick up his socks from the bottom of the stairs and put them in the wash basket,' Nina said. 'That was all.'

'Oh,' Finch said.

When he reached past Nina to fill a pint-glass with cold water, he noticed red rake marks on her arms. 'Did he do that?' he asked.

'He's just been uncontrollable all day,' she said. 'Maybe it's the heat.'

Finch took three big gulps from his glass and then

headed towards the thumping, taking the steps two at a time.

'Don't make him worse,' Nina said.

In his room, Brody was banging a felt tip pen into a black and white picture of Superman torn from a colouring book. Superman's cape and boots had been coloured-in neatly with red, but the rest of his body was the victim of a vicious felt-tip tattoo, which had torn through the paper, leaving him all chewed-up.

'Hey hey hey,' Finch said. 'Don't break your pen.'

Finch took the pen from Brody. The tip of it had split open against the floorboards. Brody growled at him, his face so red it looked swollen. Sweat was all over him, sticking his hair to his forehead, even rising in beads on the sides of his nose.

'Ssssssh,' Finch said. 'We'll get you another pen.' And then he whispered softly for Brody to calm down, to take a deep breath, reassuring him that he would listen to his side of the story.

Brody slumped down onto the bed, his arms crossed, wearing a professional pout. Finch sat next to him.

'Mummy wouldn't find me a yellow pen,' Brody said. 'And I need yellow for Superman's belt and badge.'

'Okay, well we'll find you a yellow,' Finch said. 'But did Mummy ask you to do something first, before she found you a yellow?'

'I don't want to pick up my stupid socks.'

Finch put his arm around Brody's shoulders, but the boy was too hot, his t-shirt damp and stinky.

'Let's get some fresh air in here,' Finch said. 'How can you colour with the curtains closed?'

Finch opened the curtains and window, allowing light and cool air to intrude on Brody's gloom.

With the patience of a hostage negotiator, Finch discussed with Brody the terms of their agreement, and by degrees, Brody calmed down, taking in big breaths, eventually smiling. 'When we find the yellow pen,' Brody said, 'will you help me colour-in Superman, Daddy?'

'Sure I will, sure,' Finch said. 'But first you're going to apologise to Mummy. You can't hurt her like that Brody. You cannot scratch her. You're nearly 13. Look at how strong you're getting now.'

They marched down the stairs together, Finch's hand on Brody's shoulder. In the kitchen, Brody made a remorseful curl of his lower lip and pulled on the back of Nina's shirt.

'Sorry Mummy,' he said, and held out his arms for a hug. Nina hugged back, keeping her dripping-wet washing up gloves at a distance.

'That's alright baby,' Nina said. 'Just please don't do it again.'

'I won't,' Brody said.

Finch wished he could believe it.

The three sharks performed lazy circles of the tank, the slow undulations of their tails propelling them round at an even speed, their heads moving from side to side, sniffing for some distraction from the endless conveyor.

Finch tossed three shovelfuls of bloody mackerel chunks from a washing up bowl, and where they hit, the sharks whipped up the surface into a froth with their tails.

'Don't feed them too much,' Doc Ortiz said from the doorway. 'Don't want them being boring in the morning.'

'They need a little, just to keep them keen,' Finch said, shaking Ortiz's hand when he held it out.

'So are you all set for tomorrow?' Ortiz said.

'I'm just about to pull out the regrowths. It's amazing how quick the teeth start to come back.'

'Well, I just came to give you this,' Ortiz said, holding out a soft parcel wrapped in brown paper.

'Thanks.'

'We're all going to wear them tomorrow.'

Finch unwrapped the paper, and inside was a red t-shirt

with the words 'Go Hector! Santa Carla Day 23.8.1975' stencilled on in black.

'Do you mind if I stay and watch you?' Doc Ortiz asked.

'Sure,' Finch said. He set down the shirt on the trestle table where his pistol was laid out, alongside the plastic tub of darts with the word 'Tranqs' written in faded marker on the side.

'How's that boy of yours doing?' Ortiz asked.

'He's okay,' Finch said. 'We managed to get him into The Mount last March. He's doing much better there. He gets one-on-one attention most of the day. And he likes the food better there than at the old school. He prefers their potato salad to Nina's though, and that drives her crazy.'

Ortiz laughed. 'That's good to hear. About the school I mean. And how long will he stay there?'

'Right up to eighteen. And they even have links with Alvarez College. Some of the pupils there actually do the Baccalaureate, on day release. So, you know, it's a possibility, if he's able.'

'That's great,' Ortiz said, looking down at his sandals and flexing his toes.

'I saw Hector yesterday,' Finch said.

'Yes, he said he came over. No fear that boy. He's been showing everyone the tooth you gave him.'

'Seems like a good kid.'

'We couldn't be prouder,' Ortiz said, pinching his lips together. 'You know, a friend of mine runs a farm in Salamacha. He has lots of kids like Brody there, after they've left school. They help out with the animals. He's got goats and pigs and all sorts. He teaches the kids practical skills. Stuff within their capabilities. And he pays them a fair wage for it. He's even got a minibus that goes round and picks them up. Kids like that love animals. If you like, I could give you his number. You know, something to consider for the future.'

Finch pushed a red-tailed dart into the barrel of his

pistol, aimed the sight at the tiger shark, and pulled the trigger. Ortiz flinched at the sound of the explosion. The dart hit the shark just behind the head.

'Jeez, you could have warned me,' Ortiz said.

'Sorry,' Finch said.

While he reloaded, the tiger shark turned on its side, and its momentum carried it to the edge of the pool, where its snout scraped against the curved surface, and brought it to a stop.

Ortiz held his hands over his ears while Finch fired the second shot at one of the bull sharks.

'Listen,' Ortiz said. 'I'm gonna get out of here while I've still got some of my hearing left. I'll see you in the morning.' As he was walking out the door, Ortiz turned and said, 'Remember to wear your t-shirt!' and gave Finch a big thumbs-up.

Finch tranquillised the last shark, and then set the gun back down on the trestle table. He picked up the t-shirt and tossed it in the rubbish bin.

When Finch got home, Nina was asleep on the sofa with her headphones on. The whole downstairs smelled of the chilli waiting in a pan on the stove. He went upstairs to Brody's room, leaned down to wipe the boy's damp hair from his forehead and put a kiss there. In the silence, the shock of the tranquilliser gunshot came back to him, along with Doc Ortiz's voice. *Kids like that.*

Back downstairs, Finch lit the gas beneath the pan of chilli with a match. He tipped a little salt into a saucer and ripped off small chunks of bread from a loaf to dip into it.

'Hey,' Nina said. She was leaning against the doorframe looking sleepy, her hair all over the place.

'I was trying to be quiet,' Finch said.

'I was waiting up for you.'

Finch poured red wine into two clay cups and set them on the dining table. Nina sat down and took a drink.

'So I saw Juliette today,' she said.

'And how is she?'

'She's a cow.'

'Oh.'

'Brody's been asking to hang out with Rose for weeks now, which is why I invited her over, but Juliette came without her. She said Rose didn't want to come. She went to the beach with her friends instead.'

'Was Brody okay?'

'He didn't say anything, but... it just kills me.'

'They were so sweet when they were little.'

'Yeah, well she's a bitch now. Her and her mum.'

'So what's she up to?'

'You don't want to know. It will only make you vomit.'

Finch reached across the table and squeezed Nina's hand. 'You and Brody are the only people in the world who don't make me want to vomit,' he said.

The roads around the bay were glittering, the sun reflecting off the chrome trimmings of hundreds of cars parked end-to-end all the way out of town, as far as a mile out, where a line of people carrying canvas bags and cool boxes headed for the lagoon. As they arrived, local restaurant and shop owners welcomed them, standing at the edge of their turf, alongside blackboards painted with special Santa Carla Day deals on souvenirs and drinks and ice creams. There was an air of celebration. Everyone happy.

At eight o'clock, Finch, Nina and Brody went down to the aquarium. Hundreds of visitors always came early to see the sharks before the ceremony started. Nina and Brody managed the welcome desk. Brody liked to take the coins and notes from people and sort them into the trays in the till.

Finch briefed the two extra hands he'd hired, lifeguards from the local pool, which was always closed on the day of the ceremony because they got no business. These two young lads leaned against the railings around the shark pool, answering the questions they were able to from the laminated fact sheets Finch had prepared. Their main responsibility was to make sure that no one did anything stupid, like jump in, or, as happened one year, treat the shallow pool like a wishing well and chuck coins at the sharks.

When it was time to leave, Finch stretched up to the top shelf behind the welcome desk to reach the ceremonial box, a weathered old thing with brass hinges, which at one time had held a navigator's sextant. While he kissed Nina on the lips, he felt Brody fiddling with the box, trying to open the latch.

'Not for you,' Finch said, and hugged the boy.

Down the steps, at the edge of the lagoon, where there were already hundreds of people gathered, Finch saw Hector's group, all wearing their red t-shirts. At the centre of them was Doc Ortiz, strutting around shaking hands and slapping people on the back. Hector was on the lagoon wall with his arms folded, the creases in his forehead visible from way off. His friends fought around him with water pistols.

'Where's your shirt, Finch?' Ortiz asked.

'I'm on the sharks' side,' Finch said, getting laughs from Hector's troop, but an annoyed headshake from Ortiz.

Ortiz called his son over, and even though it was Finch's job to begin the ceremony, the Doc raised his hands over his head to clap, initiating a round of applause that went the whole way round the lagoon. Local notables had already gathered around them, sponsors, prominent businessmen, elected officials, and Santa Carla Day old boys.

Finch held the ceremonial box, one hand flat on the bottom, one hand flat on the top, as it was always done, and held it out to Hector's father.

'Do you accept?' Finch said.

'I do,' Ortiz said, the grin falling from his face for a moment of appropriate solemnity. Ortiz took the box, one hand on each side, and then, hands shaking a little, opened the lid.

'Did you sterilise this?' Doc Ortiz said, taking out the pearl-handled penknife. 'You know I'd be stripped of my licence if I did a procedure with a dirty instrument.' And then he grinned to reassure everyone that he was just teasing.

Digging his thumbnail into the groove, Ortiz pulled out the blade. Good craftsmanship and decades of assiduous cleaning and oiling made this a smooth action that finished with a spring-loaded click, locking the blade in place. Excited chatter spread around the circumference of the lagoon.

'It's clean enough,' Finch said, but Doc Ortiz still made a big show of pulling out a petrol lighter, delighting the crowd as he passed the flame along the length of the blade. 'I wouldn't want him to get an infection,' Ortiz said, and there were guffaws from everyone within earshot.

'Ready?' Ortiz said. Hector nodded. 'All set Finch?'

'All set.'

The clock on the tower atop the public library showed four minutes to eleven. It was time.

'Knock 'em dead Hector,' Ortiz said. The Doc crouched down and marked an area of skin on the side of his son's thigh with his outstretched thumb and forefinger. He placed the blade against him. Hector's mother winced, both fists at her chin. Sweat gathered on Ortiz's upper lip. He drew the blade across Hector's leg in a clean confident slice. The cut was neat and long, at first releasing nothing, until the leg, as if suddenly realising it was cut, began to leak. Blood dripped down Hector's thigh, over his knee, barely diverted by tiny blond hairs.

Hector held out his hand to Finch, and Finch shook it. The boy's palm was slim and sticky.

Ortiz gave his boy the wooden paddle, a weapon gnawed ragged by decades of toothless sharks. Annual sanding and varnishing had maintained this paddle, preserving inside every layer the story of each of the town's top boys since the first ceremony in 1941, the year after the sinking of the *Santa Carla*, when sharks had set upon the town's bravest while they waited for rescue, leaving the sea empty, all 71 gone, when the rescue boats finally arrived.

Ortiz looked at the clock, now showing two and a half minutes to eleven. 'You'd better move it Finch,' he said.

Finch jogged around the edge of the lagoon, back to the aquarium. A sense memory of Hector's hand remained on his palm. He wiped his hand against his shorts, but it could not be shaken.

Looking back at the clock, Finch saw that he now had just 90 seconds left. He panicked as the bolt on the gate to the shark enclosure stuck. He pulled the iron mechanism hard enough that when it shifted and his hand flew back, it cut a rusty gash into the side of his forefinger.

Over the other side of the lagoon, Hector held the paddle above his head. It bestowed a power upon him that was tangible to everyone. His chest swelled. His chin lifted. Borne on by cheers and whistles, he stepped into the lagoon, striding thigh-deep towards the black granite stone set in the middle, his wound twirling red ribbons in the water.

The long steel handle of the enclosure's locking mechanism rattled against its fixings as the sharks bashed up against the gate, the tiger shark thwacking it with its tail, the bulls driving in with their snouts.

Earlier in the morning, when Finch had first arrived, they had been docile, mooching along with lazy waves of their long bodies. But now, already smelling the blood in the lagoon behind the gate, their vigour had returned. Since they'd been caught eight months ago off the coast of Morocco as juveniles, they'd been fed generous portions every day, building up their size, until three weeks ago when Finch began to dwindle their rations, encouraging the kind of lusty hunger that you see only in the most desperate wild sharks, the kind that risk beaching themselves in holiday resort shallows for a mouthful of leg and lilo.

The clock now showed one minute to eleven.

Hector arrived at the stone in the middle of the lagoon.

The soaked lower half of his t-shirt clung to his waist. He set both feet a steadying hip-width apart, and then, leaning forward, held the paddle in both hands the way he might a tennis racket. Even from 200 feet away on the enclosure wall, Finch could see the boy's chest rising and falling as he panted, his mouth a tight circle, his gaze on the gate.

Finch held up his hand to announce his readiness, and in response, on the other side of the lagoon, coinciding with the last sweep of the second hand on the library tower clock, Ortiz began a countdown, 'Ten! Nine!' The crowd joined in, getting louder with each count.

The sharks redoubled their efforts against the gate, so that Finch had to squeeze the handle to steady it.

'Zero!'

The bells in the clock tower began to peal.

Finch hesitated for a second, then pulled the handle.

The tiger shark muscled its way through the gate, pectoral fins scraping against the sides. The two bulls barrelled on in its wake. The boy shifted his weight from foot to foot as they came for him, clenching and unclenching his fingers on the paddle. The crowd was silent now, holding its combined breath as the sharks cut a quick path to the boy's legs, spurred on by bells whose ringing at eleven o'clock every day had announced each of the sharks' meals in captivity.

Five seconds into the bells, the crowd found its voice again as the tiger shot straight past Hector, clipping his leg and knocking him sideways. Hector's paddle-slap landed in the waves it left behind.

The crowd chanted Hector's name. As the two bulls came for him, the boy lifted the paddle high. Waiting until the last moment, he brought the chewed end down on the head of the lead shark. The bull performed a tail-twisting brake and turn, thrashing up waves which knocked Hector off balance. The second bull shark lunged in, butting him with its snout and taking his legs out from under him.

There was a collective intake of breath from the crowd as Hector went down on his hands and knees, his head submerged for a second. The tiger spun a tight circle and launched at his hip, jaws agape.

Finch's toes curled over the edge of the wall.

Hector jumped up, and in a crowd-pleasing display of acrobatics, grabbed the end of his dropped paddle, spun round, spraying water in a wide arc, and caught the tiger right across the eye with a perfect slap. The shark's eye flashed white with a protective blink and it slipped past him, undamaged.

At the end of Hector's spin, when his momentum ran out, the tiger came back at him, the water making a hollow slapping sound in the cavern of its open mouth. It turned side-on to align with Hector's waist, and when it bit, pushing Hector along hopping on one foot, the foam around him turned from white to red. The crowd gasped. Ortiz looked from his son to Finch. Finch folded his arms.

The blood drove the two bulls into a frenzy. They were all about him, tail tips and fins flashing as they took exploratory bites, heedless of the paddle's blows. One of the bulls caught his leg and held it, rolling, trying to tug him under.

The roar of the crowd deflated into anxious murmurs. There had never been blood before. Hector's father had one foot in the lagoon, and one on the wall, his hands cupped around his mouth to amplify his cries of 'Get up Hector!'

There were 20 seconds left, but already the crowd was shouting 'Get out!'

For a moment, their encouragement seemed to help, and Hector got to his feet. Half his t-shirt was torn away, revealing for the first time the crescent of puncture wounds leaking blood down his side.

Someone rang the hand-bell to signal the end of the 71 seconds, and into the silence that followed, the crowd yelled, 'Run!' But Hector was deaf to it. His eyes were bulging, lips peeled back from his teeth. Water flew from the paddle as he raised it again, and with the most perfect timing, began a fearsome downward stroke as one of the bulls leapt from the water, two-thirds of its long body breaching the surface, its jaws opened wide. Hector's sopping fringe slapped his eyes as he brought the paddle down right on top of the bull's head with all his weight. The shark hit his stomach and they both went down together.

There was nothing above the water but fins.

Finch grabbed the gun from the first aid kit and jumped into the lagoon. The water dragged at each of his strides.

Hector came up for a moment, and everyone heard the breath he snatched before the tiger crashed into him again, collapsing his lungs with an explosive pop. The sound got Ortiz moving. And now others were jumping into the lagoon too, preparing to risk their own lives, self-preservation forgotten in a wave of solidarity.

Finch was ahead of everyone else. He held the gun high above his head to keep it safe from the splashes, lowering it only when he was within shooting distance. Hector came up again, belly first, pushed forward on the top of the tiger's head. The boy's eyes were closed and his arms limp. One of the bulls slipped in from underneath and took the whole of Hector's right hand and forearm in its mouth. It tugged the boy under with a jerk that loosed a cloud of red into the water. When Hector resurfaced a moment later in the pink foam, he was face down.

The other bull shark came at Finch from the side. Finch swung the gun round to meet it. The trigger was stiff and his aim was shaky, but the bull was so close that not even Finch's timidity with the weapon could bungle the shot. His two rounds pulled screams from the crowd, exploded into the bull's grey back, drove it underwater, out of sight.

The shots sent the remaining two sharks back towards the aquarium gate. Finch emptied the last four rounds into the water round about their fleeing shadows.

Hector had been face-down in the water for too long. Finch took big leaping steps towards him, grabbed his ripped t-shirt, pulled him close, slipped both arms under the boy and lifted him up. Hector's skin was cold. Bloodied water clung about his goosebumps.

And then Ortiz was there, yowling his son's name, wresting him from Finch. Finch was vaguely aware of another man at his side, two men, all holding the boy up together, shouting instructions. Finch's ears were ringing. He looked down at his feet. He was standing on the black granite circle, and it held him there.

Ortiz and the others got Hector to the side. The crowd cleared a space around them. Ortiz clamped his open mouth over Hector's, pinched his nose, puffed air into him, inflated his chest.

The body of a dead bull shark floated beside Finch, its belly pale in the red water.

Finch watched Ortiz struggle to put air and life back into his son.

This is how hard you should have fought for my son when you brought him into the world, he thought. This hard.

Burying Chiyoko Sasaki

ACROSS THE DINING table from Nobu, his daughter Grace sat chewing a pencil. 'You've got to eat *something*,' he said, looking at the breakfast things between them, the crackers and jam, the frozen green grapes and cranberry juice.

'Why don't *you* eat something then?' she said.

After a few minutes of nothing but listening to the wind rattling tree branches against their roof tiles, Nobu nudged Grace's foot with the toe of his slipper, setting her leg swinging. 'Time to get your shoes on,' he said. From upstairs came the squeaks and thumps of his wife, Aiko, climbing out of the bath.

And then someone knocked on the front door and made Nobu jump in his seat.

Peering through the netted window beside the door, he saw a big round man in a charcoal grey suit. His head was bowed, exposing a bald circle ringed by closely shaven grey hair. With one hand he clutched his other wrist. A yellow taxi was parked on the street behind him, and when Nobu opened the door, just a few inches, he could hear that its engine was still running.

'Good morning,' the man said, with a solid bow. 'I'm sorry to call so early, but I came because I read about Chiyoko Sasaki.'

Nobu was unable to meet the man's gaze. 'It's not a good time,' he said.

The man took one step towards the door. Nobu held his

position, blocking the doorway with his body.

'I knew Chiyoko-San when I was a boy,' the man said. 'I was sad to hear she had passed, and in such a way. May I come in, just for a moment, and pay my respects?"

Nobu glanced back, into the house.

'Now is not…'

'My name is Masato Hasegawa,' the man said, reaching into his jacket pocket, and making a grunt, as if this small gesture cost him some effort. He took out a silver case, and from it plucked a business card. Nobu took the card and recognised on it the logo that appeared on a prominent black-glass building in the city. The building had an impressive shape, like a sail. Beneath Masato's name on the card, it said 'Director'. Nobu opened the door further.

'I'm Nobu Sasaki,' he said. 'Chiyoko was my great-grandmother.'

'I grew up in this area,' Masato said, looking round for a moment at the leafy street behind him. The taxi turned off its engine. Three girls on bicycles rang their bells as they passed. 'I've not been back here in a long time.'

Masato stood just looking at Nobu. Nobu had no choice but to open the door fully. 'We're in the middle of getting ready,' he said. 'The house is a mess I'm afraid.'

'I won't stay long. I just want to visit Chiyoko-San's shrine, if I may?'

The leather of Masato's shoes creaked as he shifted his great weight forward. Nobu hesitated for a second, then stepped aside to allow Masato in.

'Can I get you some tea or coffee?'

'No no no,' Masato said, shaking his head and raising his hands. 'I don't want to be any bother.'

Masato bent down to remove his shoes and set them together beside the door. His socks were purple. As Masato stood, Nobu noticed him stare for a moment at his own suede slippers, the poor condition of which revealed many years of wear and dozens of spillages.

Masato came into the house, keeping his hands locked respectfully before him. Grace stared at him, opening her mouth slightly and leaving it that way until the pencil unstuck itself from her lips and fell, clattering on the table. Masato nodded at her and smiled.

'I'm sorry I came so early, Mr Sasaki,' Masato said. 'My job means the only spare minutes I get are first and last thing.'

'It's good of you to come,' Nobu said. He tried to shoo Grace away with a stern look and a flick of his hand, but she remained, poking a stippled pattern into the skin of a frozen grape with the tip of her pencil.

'It's just through here,' Nobu said. He led Masato into the living room, to the altar, which he, Aiko and Grace had constructed last night. They'd draped white cloth over a bench and two tall boxes to make a series of steps. On these steps and either side of them they had arranged many colourful flowers, two watermelons, a pineapple, a ceramic cup of red wine, candles and incense holders, a stack of hardback novels tied together with white ribbon, and a black and white photograph in a silver frame of Chiyoko Sasaki, old, unsmiling, upright on a chair in a photographer's studio.

To the side of the altar, the doors of the family shrine were shut and sealed over with white paper. Just as Nobu motioned for Masato to go ahead, he noticed a streak of graphite on this paper, and at its darkest end, a tear. He shuddered.

'Is it okay if I wash my hands?' Masato asked.

'Just one second,' Nobu said, hurrying to the kitchen area to empty the dirty crockery from the sink and stack it on the draining board. He tapped the table in front of Grace just once, leaving a wet fingerprint, and said, 'Go get ready.' She pushed her chair away from the table, curled forwards, then fell onto her hands and knees, crawling under the table and up the stairs with theatrical slowness.

'Come through,' Nobu said to Masato, beckoning him over.

Masato took off his chunky silver watch and placed it to the side of the sink before pulling up his sleeves as high as his thick forearms would allow. He was a hairy man, the grey fur ending at his wrists.

Nobu stood an appropriate distance from Masato's back while he washed his hands, and looked around as if for the first time at the condition of his home: the side of the sofa shredded by a cat that was long gone, the broken blind in the dining room that could not be opened, Grace's dirty gym kit draped over the bannister, and the cardboard recycling heaped beside the back door.

'Your great-grandmother was my violin teacher,' Masato said. He turned off the tap and shook his wet fingers into the sink, looking around for a towel.

'One moment,' Nobu said.

He ran upstairs, and as he passed Grace's bedroom, saw her sitting on the floor peeling off one of her school socks. 'What are you doing?' he said.

'They don't match,' she said, holding the sock up and pushing forward with her thumbs the embroidered pink rabbit.

He came close to her, kneeling down to speak quietly. 'There's a tear in the paper over the shrine. Did *you* do it?'

'No.'

'Look at your *face*,' he said. 'I can *tell* you're lying.'

'I am not!'

Nobu took in a big breath and rubbed his face with both hands. 'Just hurry up,' he said.

In the linen cupboard Nobu rummaged through the tightly packed sheets until he found a small hand towel, then ran back downstairs to Masato, handing it to him still folded.

'She was an amazing person,' Masato continued, drying each of his fingers in turn. 'Very patient. I was a sloppy pupil. But she demanded total concentration from me.'

'She could be very strict,' Nobu said.

'When I was young, my mind was always floating off. The tiniest distraction could lure it away from whatever I was supposed to be working on. I could be lost for ages, just gazing at nothing in particular. Chiyoko-San would pinch me, right here, on the underside of the arm, whenever I lost my concentration. It hurt like crazy.' Masato laughed.

'I know that pinch well,' Nobu said.

'And always in the same spot! But I have her to thank for tethering my mind to the world of real things. I wouldn't hold the position I hold today if it wasn't for your great-grandmother. I owe her so much. I feel guilty that it's taken me so long to come back here. I spent so many hours after school in this house. I should have visited her while she was alive. I meant to, many times. But you know how work gets in the way.'

Nobu nodded and took the towel back from Masato. Masato clipped his watch round his wrist and pulled his cuffs back into position, refastening the buttons. Back at the altar, he hoisted up his trouser legs a little and knelt on the floor mat. His knees made a popping sound. Seeming to lose his breath for a moment, he sucked in a big ball of air through his nose, then tore a match from the little book, lit an incense stick and placed it in the brass holder, alongside the others. He bowed his head, and once he had his breathing back under control, was silent.

Nobu could not help but stare at Masato's bright socks. He could hear Aiko and Grace talking upstairs, and then Aiko's footsteps along the landing. She paused a moment before coming down, her bare feet and calves coming into Nobu's view first, and then her towelling dressing gown. She stopped on the bottom step, splashing droplets of water from her long hair as she rubbed it with her fingers. Nobu shook his head to stop her, tiptoed over, and in the softest whisper, warned her about the visitor. Aiko held onto the bannister and balanced on the ball of one foot to swing round and look into the near corner. Masato stood and turned, bowing to her.

Aiko smiled and nodded in return, pulling her gown close around her neck.

'Hi,' she said. 'You knew Chiyoko-San I hear.'

'I did,' Masato said. 'I was just telling your husband about her violin lessons.'

'Ahhh. Do you still play?'

'I do,' Masato smiled, looking to the ground. 'But I have no real talent.'

Aiko laughed. 'Did my husband tell you that Chiyoko refused to teach him because he was so terrible?'

'He didn't,' Masato said.

'I knew Chiyoko before I knew Nobu,' Aiko said. 'She and my grandma were best friends. I know she only took on pupils who had a real gift, so maybe you're just being humble.'

Masato flushed. 'Whatever ability I had, it was nothing compared to hers.'

'Well, it was good to meet you. I must go and get ready.'

'Sorry, before you go,' Masato said, stopping Aiko on the stairs. 'I read in the paper about the wake here tomorrow, and I wanted to ask you both if I could play, in honour of Chiyoko-San?'

Nobu looked at Aiko, and she smiled. 'We'd love that,' she said, then made her farewells and headed back upstairs.

When Masato and Nobu were alone again, Masato said, 'You're a lucky man. You have a lovely family.'

'Thanks.' Nobu took a step in the direction of the front door, as if to subtly herd Masato towards it.

'We have three children and five grandchildren,' Masato said. 'But they all live far away, and we only get to see them a few times a year. I miss having them around.'

'I can't imagine Grace grown up and moved out,' Nobu said.

'You have just one child?'

'Yes.'

'Enjoy every moment. One day you wake up and they've become adults, so suddenly, like it happened while you were asleep.' Masato looked around, at Aiko's bead pictures of imaginary birds on the walls, and at the ceiling, the nicotine yellow of which bled through every coat of paint eventually. 'It must have been awfully quiet here when Chiyoko was gone. I imagine it was especially hard on your daughter.'

'Grace never knew her,' Nobu said. 'She went missing while Grace was still a baby.'

'A terrible shame. But at least a little relief now, I suppose, that you can lay her to rest. How long was she gone?'

'Twelve years,' Nobu said. 'She might have stayed undiscovered forever, if it wasn't for that poor girl.'

'Yes,' Masato said, shaking his head. 'It must have been agony for her parents, to see her pulled out of the water like that.'

'She was only a couple of years older than Grace is now. It's frightening. That spot on the lake was always my family's favourite.'

'How old would Chiyoko have been at the time of her passing? She was already grey when I was a boy. She must have been well on her way to a hundred.'

'She was ninety, I think. She always lied about her age, in both directions, so we were never completely sure.'

'Impressive, considering she always had a cigarette in her hand. And are your parents still around?'

'No, I lost them both when I was very young.'

'I'm sorry.'

'I was brought up by my grandparents. Chiyoko outlived them both.'

'She certainly was tenacious.'

'Yes.'

They stood there without speaking for a moment, Masato looking around at the house and nodding to himself,

Nobu listening to the sounds from upstairs of Aiko replacing the cap of her lipstick, and Grace zipping up her school bag.

At the door, before he left, Masato bowed and thanked Nobu again for his hospitality. Nobu watched him walk down the path, so buffeted by the wind he could barely keep a straight line. Just before he reached the gate, Masato stopped and came back a few steps. 'Sorry,' he said. 'I should have asked. Is there any piece in particular that you'd like me to play at the wake tomorrow, something that was special to Chiyoko-San?'

'No,' Nobu said. 'Play whatever you like.'

Long after Masato was gone, and Grace had caught the bus to school, and Aiko had cycled to the shops, he still wished that he had not said it quite like that.

Masato's presence in the house had alerted Nobu to its improper state for holding a wake. Early that evening, while Aiko tended to steaming pans on all six of the hob's burners, Nobu went round the house tightening screws on wonky cupboard doors, he taped over the tear in the shrine's paper covering, and worked up a sweat on his hands and knees, washing the floor with an old pillow case and a bucket of hot soapy water.

In the living room, Grace practised on her upright piano. Masato's request to play violin at the wake had inspired Aiko to ask her daughter whether she would play something, too. She had been reluctant, complaining that she was rusty, having played less than a couple of hours during the whole of the summer holidays, but she relented when Nobu said she could be excused from cleaning duties.

'He kept asking questions,' Nobu said as he scrubbed the tiles around Aiko's feet.

'So what?'

'There's something weird about him.' Nobu wrung grey-brown water from the pillowcase.

'I thought he seemed nice.'

'No one who liked Chiyoko so much can be that nice.'

'He's just coming to play the violin.'

'As if it's not going to be stressful enough tomorrow.'

'I'm actually looking forward to it,' Aiko said.

'How *can* you be?'

'Soon we get to move on. After tomorrow, there's just the funeral to get through, and then we make a fresh start.'

'I hope you're right,' Nobu said. 'I hope that's how it will be.'

Nobu waited until 3am, and then gave up trying to sleep. In the dark, he rummaged on the floor beside the bed for his dressing gown, being careful not to disturb Aiko, who lay beside him with the duvet bunched up between her legs. He always joked that she became an ogre if woken before daybreak.

He crept along the landing and had got to the top of the stairs when he heard something out of place. A sound like a tap left running. He checked the bathroom, but the taps were tight. Following this sound a slow footstep at a time, he came to Grace's half-open door. The orange light that fell in through the gap in her curtains sparkled on her open eyes.

'What are you doing awake?' he whispered, coming into her room and sitting on the edge of her bed. She pulled out the earbud headphones, making the strange sound loud enough now for him to recognise it as music. The light from the screen of her iPod filled up the space between them with a warm blue glow.

'I can't sleep,' she said.

'Thinking about tomorrow?' he asked.

She shrugged.

'I was going to make some tea,' Nobu said. 'Do you want something?'

She shook her head.

'I'm sorry about the paper,' she said.

Nobu patted the back of her hand. 'It's a silly superstition,' he said. 'I'm sorry for the way I reacted.'

'I don't want to play the piano tomorrow.'

'You're going to be great,' he said. 'Now get some sleep.' He kissed her forehead, and then saw on her bedside table a tin foil dragonfly. 'How did this break?' Nobu asked, picking it up and turning it over lightly.

'It just fell off,' she said. They both looked up at the mobile in front of her window. Even though the window was closed, the draught was strong enough to set in motion the other 11 dragonflies.

'I remember making each one of these,' Nobu said.

'I know,' she said.

Guests' shoes quickly filled up the small tiled area by the front door and spilled out in a neat centipede along the dining room wall. Grace greeted the guests at the door, gratefully receiving each of their white envelopes and setting them on a specially prepared table. Each time she opened the door, she kept herself behind it, as she had been instructed, to avoid the lenses of the three photographers that were leaning against their low fence.

Aiko would not let Nobu hide in the kitchen, where he was re-washing clean glasses, even when he admitted he was terrified that if he were to speak, he might let slip some accidentally damning statement to fuel the suspicions of these nosy old acquaintances from so long ago, most of whom he was certain had not even known Chiyoko, but had heard on the news about her gruesome discovery and were here out of ghoulish curiosity. Aiko gave Nobu his jacket, despite the heat in the house, and led him by the elbow to be among them.

He worried about the moment of Masato's arrival, and wondered why this man, who'd seemed like the type to be strictly punctual, was late. But then he saw that Masato was already there, kneeling once more before the altar, his violin case at his side. Today, his socks were grass-green.

At the moment the priest arrived and stepped across the threshold, the atmosphere thickened. The silence this old man brought with him amplified the creaking of the house. Nobu stared at his long eyebrows and listened to the dreadful scraping of his white robes on the floor mats.

When the prayers were finished, the air in the house was thick with floral incense. Nobu got to his feet and headed to the garden for fresh air. He weaved through people, his head lowered so he could avoid being stopped. He felt sick to be among them, and longed for a moment later that day when the house would again be his, and he could shed his suit, put his bare feet on the table and hold a cold bottle of beer against his forehead.

Aiko complained to Nobu that people were using the paper plates to fan themselves, and were not eating. Soon the heat in the house would spoil the food that she had spent the night preparing. She slid open the windows beside the shrine at one end of the room, while he opened the big double doors at the other, allowing the wind to blow through. The tunnel of air pulled all the incense smoke through the house and cast it outside. One big gust caused the apple-heavy branches of the tree in the back garden to thump the lawn, making everyone look.

Although Nobu and Aiko did not know what level of proficiency Masato held at the violin, they thought it best, just in case he was good, that their daughter perform on the piano first. Nobu watched her through the open doors to the garden, his jacket over his arm, enjoying the way the wind fluttered his shirt. In the corner, three women talked the whole way through Grace's faltering performance of *The Swan*, from Saint Saens' *The Carnival of the Animals.* No amount of glaring at the back of their heads would shut them up.

What vexed him even more was that later, when Masato unpacked his violin and took position beside the altar, the first perfect note he pulled from the violin's small scuffed body silenced them all and turned every head.

Nobu didn't recognise the music, but it was a sad piece, full of high long-held notes and deep silences. Masato's eyes were closed the whole time, the violin rest pressed into his fat chin. Although his feet remained planted, he swayed the same way Chiyoko always had, as if charmed by his own music, the emotion of the piece rendered in his face, which was a shifting canvas of grief. It was almost unbearable to watch.

Later, from outside, came the sound of a dropped wine glass smashing on the garden decking. Nobu ushered everyone back inside so he could sweep up the fragments with a dustpan and brush. Grateful for this distraction, he worked assiduously, fine-tuning his eyes for the tiniest splinters of glass. From this stooped position, Nobu suddenly became aware of Masato's green socks at the edge of his vision.

'Sorry to disturb you,' Masato said.

'Your playing was...amazing,' Nobu said.

'I'm nothing but the instrument of my teacher.'

'So, do you play professionally?'

'No,' he laughed. 'Just for pleasure. I've not played in front of people like that since I was young. I'm afraid my fingers were quite clumsy with nerves.'

'You're kidding, right?' Nobu said. 'You were perfect. I've not seen Aiko cry like that in...' and then he remembered the circumstances of the last few weeks, and realised that he had spoken foolishly, so stopped himself there. He tipped the pan back and shook it to shuffle the glass fragments close together.

'I wanted to talk with you about something,' Masato said.

Nobu scratched his throat.

'I'm afraid I have to...'

'I'll only keep you a moment.' Masato gestured towards the bench beneath the apple tree. Nobu followed him there, putting the pan of glass on the floor beside him. The bench was small, forcing the two men to sit close together. From here, Nobu could see the guests inside the house setting their empty glasses on the table and beginning to leave.

'I wanted to ask you two things, if I may,' Masato said.

Nobu nodded. He was breaking a fresh sweat.

'I'm filled with guilt,' Masato said.

'What do *you* have to feel guilty about?'

'Since I read about Chiyoko-San's death, the times I spent with her when I was a child have been coming back to me so vividly. I've been realising quite how important she was to me. I've had many teachers in my life, but none like her. She was special. I owe her so much, and I've dishonoured her by staying away all this time.'

'You shouldn't feel guilty about that. She had lots of students and you're the first to come back.'

'That makes me sad. It's quite obvious to me now how life might have been different if I'd stayed in contact with Chiyoko. As I said, she kept me tethered to the real world, but, I think, maybe I tethered myself to the wrong things. She would have seen that. I wish I could have spoken with her as an adult. A few words from her over a pot of tea could have taken my life in a quite different direction. Life with my own family might be more...'

Masato stared at the ground, his thoughts showing only in the twitching of his closed lips. Nobu listened to the far away sounds of Aiko bidding people goodbye, of Grace in her bedroom, drumming with pencils on her desk to an unfamiliar pop song. The wind set the silver dragonflies in her open window spinning, and brought over from next door the smell of soup cooking.

'My first request,' Masato said, 'is that you give me the address of your family's grave. I'd like to make a habit of visiting Chiyoko-San regularly.'

'Sure,' Nobu said. Although he worried for a moment that this might cause them to meet each other at the graveside on anniversaries.

'Thank you,' Masato said. 'My second request is about your daughter.'

'Grace?' Nobu said, sitting up straight now.

'I heard her play today,' Masato said.

'We're very proud of her.'

'She has no talent for the piano.'

Nobu coughed.

'Her hands are too small,' Masato continued. 'They're like Chiyoko's. Delicate, nimble fingers perfectly formed for the neck of a fiddle. She'll always struggle if you make her stick with the piano, but on the violin, she could be... well, we'll see if she has inherited something of Chiyoko's skill.'

'I see,' Nobu said. 'Well thanks for pointing that out, I'll...'

'I'd like to teach Grace,' Masato said.

Nobu shook his head and made a nervous laugh. 'That's very kind of you,' he said, 'but really, we...'

'I wouldn't charge anything. It would be my pleasure. And it would allow me to repay to the Sasaki family a little of what Chiyoko-San was kind enough to give to me.'

'I don't...'

'*Please*,' Masato said, putting his hand on Nobu's arm. 'It wouldn't put you in my debt at all. The debt is mine to repay.'

'We're just...'

'I'd need to visit twice a week. It would have to be at the weekends. I'm sure between us we could find a suitable time, couldn't we?'

'Well...'

'It wouldn't be an imposition. I'd get as much from spending time with Grace as she from me. My own grandchildren are so far away. I'd be a good teacher. I had the best.'

'Your offer is very generous Mr Hasegawa, but I'll need to discuss this with my wife, and with Grace, before I make any decisions.'

'Of course, yes,' Masato said. 'Let me suggest this. I'll come back this weekend, on Saturday night, and we'll have a trial lesson, to see how this arrangement would be for us all. Would six o'clock be convenient?'

'I'm not...'

'I have a spare violin at home, which Grace could borrow. I'd expect half an hour's practise from her every day before school, without distractions. That's the minimum Chiyoko-San insisted upon for me.'

'We already have a violin in the house. The one that Chiyoko used to play.'

Masato put both his hands over his mouth to hide a smile. When he blinked, he pushed tears from his eyes that spilled down his cheeks.

On their way back through the house, where the last few guests were leaving, Masato said, 'If Chiyoko's violin hasn't been played in a while, it will need some restoration work. Please let me take care of it. I know someone who is *very* good.'

Nobu went upstairs, to the wardrobe where the violin was kept, in the stuffy room at the end of the corridor that was still so heavy with Chiyoko's presence he could not bear to be in there for more than a few hurried seconds, holding his breath the whole time.

At the door, when Nobu returned, Masato was bowing to Aiko. Aiko wrapped her arms around the big man, her hands unable to meet by some distance. She squeezed Masato, which at first seemed to alarm him, but then made him smile so widely that all of his straight little teeth were revealed. 'Your playing made this a very special day,' Aiko said.

'It was an honour. Thank *you* for allowing me to play.'

Nobu passed the black violin case to Masato, and he

received it with both hands and a deep bow, as if this were more than just her instrument.

'How lovely,' Aiko said. 'I'm sure she would be so happy for you to have it.'

'No no no,' Masato said, waving his hand. 'Just borrowing for a few days. Your husband will explain.' He winked at Nobu.

Nobu and Aiko stood in the doorway to watch him leave. The photographers were gone. The wind had heaped a drift of rose petals against the fence.

'It's almost over,' Aiko said, sighing, resting her head against his arm.

'No,' Nobu said. 'It will never be over.'

Earthquakes

Mrs Sample
Sample Road
Sample Town
Sampleshire
XXXX XXX
Xx February 20xx

DEAR MRS SAMPLE,

I hope you don't mind me writing to you about my little boy, Toby. He's nine, and he has a very rare brain condition called Sterna's Syndrome. It has some unusual side effects. At the moment, there is no cure.

We only found out last year. It's every mum's worst nightmare, to hear those words. All you can think is, 'Am I going to lose my little boy?'

Since Toby got diagnosed, the Sterna's Trust has been so supportive. I'm sure you can imagine how desperate we've been for some good news, so you'll understand how excited I was when they got in touch last week to tell me that Professor Straumberg has submitted a proposal for a new research project that could eventually lead to a cure for Toby, and all the other children out there fighting Sterna's.

The Sterna's Trust is the only charity in the world that funds specific research into Sterna's Syndrome.

I feel ashamed, asking for your help, but Professor Straumberg's project is going to cost £480,000, and I just can't raise it alone.

Please will you help me find a cure for my little boy, Toby, by making a gift today of £25 to the Sterna's Trust?

I couldn't bear it if they had to say no to Professor Straumberg's research project. Right now, it's the best chance Toby has got of living a normal life. Please will you help?

Time is not on our side. No child with Sterna's Syndrome has ever lived to see their thirteenth birthday.

Toby doesn't know yet how serious his illness is. He's too young to understand, and I don't want to worry him. But in the next few years, once his Sterna's begins to get worse, I'll have to explain.

How do you tell your child something like that? How do you help them understand? I sometimes wonder whether it would be better not to tell him.

Already Toby has started talking about what he wants to be when he grows up. It breaks my heart.

Professor Straumberg's research is the only chance Toby has got of becoming an adult and living his dreams. Please will you make a gift today of £25 to the Sterna's Trust so they can say yes to Professor Straumberg's potentially life-saving research project?

Toby has already been through so much. Too much for an eight-year-old.

It all began when he was four. My husband, Jon, and I were downstairs watching a film when the house rumbled. It was like a truck going past outside, but there was no noise of a truck's engine. Just the rumbling. It made our wine glasses on the table rattle against each other. Jon and I jumped up. We never get earthquakes here, but we wondered what else it could be. It lasted ten seconds, and then we heard a noise from upstairs. A little cough.

I thought the tremor must have woken Toby up and he was scared. Jon paused the movie, and I went to check on him. By the time I got to the bottom of the stairs, I could hear another sound, like panting. My heart started thumping and I leapt up the stairs. I could just tell something was wrong.

When I got into his room, even in the dark I could see the bedclothes moving violently. Toby was making an awful gagging noise.

I tripped over trying to get to him so quickly. I switched on his light and could see that he had vomited. It was all over the floor and his bed. I screamed for Jon to come up and he came charging up the stairs.

We whipped Toby's duvet off and put him onto his side. The recovery position was the only thing I could think to do, to stop him choking. 'Call the ambulance,' I said, and Jon ran back downstairs to get the phone. I was calling Toby's name, trying to get him to hear me. He was twitching, his whole body. His eyes were wide open, almost bulging. He looked terrified, absolutely terrified. His skin was hot and his pyjamas were soaked.

I screamed for Jon to tell them to hurry up.

Jon came back into the room. He was on the phone to the ambulance people. 'Is he breathing?' Jon asked. He was relaying questions from the emergency services.

I put my ear to Toby's mouth. 'I can't tell,' I said. Toby's teeth were clamped shut. I just kept calling his name. I wanted him to stop it. I just wanted it to stop. He looked so petrified.

'Is he responding to his name?' Jon asked.

'No,' I said. 'Stop asking questions just get them here now.'

I noticed that Toby's lips were blue. The house rumbled again, and the books on Toby's shelf fell over and slid off.

'They say we've got to get him downstairs,' Jon said.

I picked Toby up. He was soaked. His whole bed was soaked.

'They want to know how long it's been going,' Jon said.

I was trying to hold him while walking down the stairs. He was still twitching in my arms and there was saliva and vomit leaking out of the side of his mouth.

When we got him on the living room floor, Jon said, 'Has he got anything trapped in his mouth?'

'How do I tell?' I asked.

'Put your finger in there,' Jon said.

But I couldn't put my finger in his mouth because he was biting his teeth together so hard.

'How long has he been going?' Jon asked. I was yelling and crying for them to get here now. I thought he was going to die. When I put my hand on his chest, his heart was galloping.

Jon opened the front door and was standing out in the street waiting for the ambulance. I was there alone with him, saying his name over and over.

Toby was making a moaning sound while he was twitching, like he was trapped inside, and petrified, and trying to communicate. 'It's okay honey,' I said, 'it's going to be okay.' I was stroking his soaking wet hair, whispering sssssshhh, trying to get him to calm down. 'It's okay baby,' I said. There was stuff coming out of his mouth and nose and I wiped it away with the sleeve of my shirt.

Suddenly Jon said, 'They're here.' I heard the sound of the engine coming closer, and then saw the blue lights flashing on the wall.

Two ambulance people came in, a man and a woman. They asked his name, and I told them it was Toby. The man said, 'Toby, can you hear me mate?'

The man pulled one of Toby's eyelids wide open and shined a little torch onto his eye. 'How long has he been like this?' the ambulance man said. I told him it was about 20 minutes, maybe more, but I didn't know. I wondered whether it might have started before we'd even heard the noise. I felt so guilty that I'd not been in the room with him. He'd felt a little warm earlier that day, but he said he felt fine when he went to bed. I felt so guilty that I wasn't there with him. My baby.

The ambulance woman opened up a big toolbox of medical gear. She had a clipboard, and the two of them started discussing medication amounts, asking how old he was, how much he weighed.

'We're going to have to cut these off him,' the man said, meaning his pyjamas.

I said that was fine. Jon was standing in the doorway with his hands on his face.

The ambulance man took a pair of scissors from a plastic packet and cut the whole way up both of Toby's pyjama legs. Toby looked so little and vulnerable, with his legs bare like that. The man rolled him onto his side, and the woman had a little pouch of medicine with a nozzle on the end. She put some jelly onto the end of it then put it into his bottom.

'Can I put a blanket on him?' I asked, and the man said I could. Toby had weed all over the floor and the front door was open. I didn't want him to be cold. I thought he might stop shaking if he was warm.

The ambulance crew phoned the hospital and said we were coming in, and they asked Jon if he was alright to carry Toby into the ambulance.

I rode in the ambulance with Toby strapped into the bed. Jon drove in the car behind. Toby's shaking had calmed down a little bit, but he was still going. The ambulance woman sat in the back with me. She asked questions about Toby, just normal questions, like did he go to playgroup and things like that.

At the hospital, when he was in the emergency room, he was still twitching. They put a cannula into the back of his hand and put more medication into him, morphine, or something like morphine, to relax his muscles.

In the end, it took over an hour to stop his seizure. I was so relieved he had stopped, but he still hadn't woken up. They'd had to give him so many drugs, they said it would take him a while to sleep them off. 'He's been through a lot,' they said.

They moved him into the children's ward. Jon and I stayed in the room with him, me sleeping on a fold-out bed and Jon on a reclining armchair in the corner. We barely slept though. We'd nod off for a few minutes at a time. The nurses came in every half hour to check on Toby, and every time, I asked if he was doing okay, and they said, 'He's doing very well.'

I didn't think he was going to wake up. It was so cold in the room. I just watched him the whole time. He was so still now. I put my finger in his little hand, but he didn't squeeze back. I worried that even if he did wake up, he would be changed. The ambulance woman said if he'd inhaled any vomit he could get an infection in his lungs, and if he'd been deprived of oxygen, it could cause brain damage.

At about six thirty, Toby opened his eyes. Jon and I were right there. He looked normal, like he was just waking up on a normal morning. He said, 'Where am I Mummy?' And Jon and I both burst out crying and hugged him. I was so relieved. I thought we'd lost him.

Afterwards, when the doctor came round before checking us out, he said most people have one seizure at some point in their lifetime. 'You get one for free,' he said. He said they can often be caused by fevers, especially in children of Toby's age. I said that Toby had been slightly warm earlier in the day, but not a temperature. He'd not been hot enough to need Calpol or anything. But the doctor didn't seem to think it mattered. To him it was all just okay. But then, when he was filling in the form, he started writing in there that the seizure was ten minutes long, and I said, no, it was over an hour. And he didn't believe me. He was acting like I didn't know what I was talking about.

We left the hospital, but I felt like Toby hadn't been properly checked, like something important hadn't been communicated between the night staff and the day staff. But

I just wanted to get home, to put it all behind us and pray that the doctor had been right, that this was Toby's one seizure and it would never happen again.

But then two days later, he had another one. Just after bedtime. Again we called the ambulance, and again it took the hospital just over an hour to stop it.

And then he had another one the day after that. One minute he was sitting on the living room floor playing with Lego, the next minute, he was curled up, twitching. They always seem to come at night, around bedtime.

It was during his third seizure that I noticed that the rumbling happened again. It caused a vase of flowers to drop off the mantelpiece and smash on the slate tiles round the fire.

I mentioned it to the ambulance crew when they arrived. I said I thought maybe it was the tremors that were causing the seizures. They gave me a look like I was a bit odd, and just carried on strapping the oxygen mask to Toby's face. But I knew there was a connection. I was looking for any patterns, anything that might be a trigger, anything to understand what was happening to my little boy.

Because of the way the ambulance man had looked at me, I didn't mention the tremors to the doctors in the hospital. I felt a bit daft. Maybe I was crazy. But then, when Toby had his fourth seizure the next week, I paid special attention to see if it would happen again.

Because his seizures were so severe, the hospital had given us the medicine to stop it, buccal midazolam. We had to keep it with us at all times so we could give it to him ourselves the second a seizure started without having to wait for the ambulance to arrive. The buccal midazolam came in little pre-prepared syringes. We had to squeeze the liquid into the corners of his mouth if he had one again and rub his cheek against his gums to get it into his bloodstream.

The dangers of Toby getting brain damage were high, because the seizures lasted so long. The consultant at the hospital said that the quicker we got the buccal midazolam into him, the better chance we'd have of stopping it turning into a really major one. So far, all the seizures had lasted more than an hour. Permanent damage can happen at anything longer than 20 minutes.

The average tonic-clonic seizure (one where the person goes stiff and starts twitching) lasts 1–3 minutes. There is a rare form of tonic-clonic seizures called status epilepticus, which are 30 minutes or longer. Even at the severe end of the seizure scale, Toby's seizures were extreme.

The fourth seizure, which was the first one where we were able to give Toby the drugs ourselves as soon as it started, lasted only 40 minutes. Now that we'd seen three, Jon and I were already getting into a kind of routine. It was still terrifying, but we knew what to expect, so it wasn't a shock the way the first one had been. It meant I could be conscious of other stuff going on in the room.

Toby was in our bed. By now, he was sleeping with me in our room every night, and Jon was sleeping downstairs on the sofa-bed. Toby couldn't be alone for a second. It happened in the middle of the night, about 2:30am. I wasn't asleep. I'd barely slept since his first one. He made a little moaning sound, and seemed to be awake for a second. He said he was okay when I asked, but then his eyes started looking off to the right hand side, and his head started flicking in the same direction. He wouldn't respond when I asked him again if he was okay. I called down to Jon to phone the ambulance, and was whispering to Toby that everything would be alright while I took the syringe out of its plastic tube. By now, we knew to try and calm Toby down. Yelling his name when he had the first seizure was probably the worst thing to do. It would only have panicked him more.

So I put the syringe into the corner of Toby's mouth and squeezed in half of the liquid, and then I did the other side. When I put the empty syringe on the bedside table it started slowly drifting sideways. I put my hand on the table top and could feel it vibrating, like it was humming. I heard a pair of my earrings rattle as they fell down the back. And then the rumbling grew strong enough that I could feel it shaking the bed. It lasted maybe ten seconds, and afterwards I knew I hadn't imagined it because the lampshade was still swinging.

Jon must have felt the tremor, too, but he denied it. He doesn't like to think about anything that's different. He doesn't even believe in taking vitamins for goodness sake. So I started doing my research without telling him.

It didn't take long to find the Sterna's Trust website. They'd designed it so that people like me could find it as soon as they started Googling anything to do with epilepsy and objects moving.

Sterna's Syndrome, the website said, is named after Henry Sterna. He lived in Bristol in the 1880s. He would have episodes where he'd talk strangely, or fall on the floor and shake, and things, even people, in a small circle around him, would fall down too. Back in those days, people had funny ideas about epilepsy. His parents were afraid of him. They packed up their things one night and left him. It breaks my heart to think of him waking up to find the house empty.

I would never let my Toby down. Please help me do everything I can for my little boy by making a gift of £25 to the Sterna's Trust today. You will make the next phase of Professor Straumberg's research into Sterna's Syndrome possible.

It was Professor Straumberg who first discovered and named Sterna's Syndrome. His own son, Klaus, had it. Klaus's seizures would make metal objects become hot. There is a photo on the Sterna's website of Professor Straumberg's wrist, which has a scar burned into it by his watchstrap. Klaus Straumberg only lived to the age of nine.

Even though modern medication has got much better at controlling seizures, the particular seizures you get with Sterna's are so long and severe that each one causes more damage in the brain, making the seizures more extreme, more frequent and harder to control. The effects build and build until the body can't take it anymore. That's why no one with Sterna's has made it into their teens yet.

When I saw all this on the Sterna's website, I was terrified, but in a way I was also relieved. At least there was an explanation. At least someone knew what was happening to Toby.

Professor Straumberg's email address was listed on the site. I wrote to him straight away and he replied that same night. He asked us to come and see him in Prague immediately.

We all went together, Toby, Jon and me. None of us had ever been to the Czech Republic before. It was December, and the Christmas markets were all out. It had snowed there. It was deep like we don't get here anymore. Toby loved that.

Professor Straumberg's clinic overlooked a little park where there were 12 snowmen all facing in the same direction. When he led us up the stairs to his office, smiling and asking us about normal things, like how was our journey, I just felt this overwhelming sense of hope. After all the frightening things I'd read about Sudden Unexpected Death in Epilepsy, worrying that I was going to lose Toby, Professor Straumberg made me feel just a little bit safer. He had an aura of calmness about him.

He asked Toby lots of questions first, before he asked us anything. This felt like a good sign. He wanted to know if Toby got any feelings in his body before a seizure happened. Toby said sometimes his hand feels funny. Professor Straumberg wanted to know a lot of detail, was it always the same hand (his right), was the feeling a numb feeling, or prickly, or hot or cold, and was it more in the fingertips or the palm? We spent the whole day there. It was exhausting, but his thoroughness was reassuring.

He answered all of my questions, and was kind enough to get one of the nurses to take Toby out into the park to make a snowman so we could speak openly.

We asked Professor Straumberg how many other children he's known about with Sterna's. He said he has examined 17, from all over the world. Right now, six other children are under his care. One of them, a little boy called Nicholas Harrison who's a year older than Toby, lives in the UK too, in Edinburgh. Professor Straumberg gave us his mum's contact details, so we could get in touch with her.

He was very frank with us. He said that very little is known about Sterna's. He's the only person in the world who specialises in it. A few decades ago, other types of epilepsy were uncontrollable, before drugs like levetiracetam, sodium valproate and lamotrigine were approved. These drugs cannot stop Sterna's seizures, the way they can some other types of seizure, but in a particular combination, Professor Straumberg has found that they can reduce the number of episodes, although not the severity when they do happen.

Seizures cause other seizures, so the more you have, the more you have, if you see what I mean. Making Toby's seizures a little less frequent would eventually lead to longer and longer spaces between them.

At the time, Toby was having two seizures a week, so we were on constant alert. I was hopeful that even if the seizures couldn't be stopped, that at least Toby might get a break between them. They're so intense, it takes him days to recover. He has dreadful headaches, and he vomits for a whole day afterwards. His muscles hurt where he's pulled them all, he's been that tensed up during an episode.

Professor Straumberg asked us what dosages Toby was on, and said he would contact our consultant back home to adjust the medication – he recommended tripling the amount of levetiracetam he is on. He also said he's had good results with a large dose of steroids given in pulses – every three days. No one knows why steroids help to reduce major seizures, but they do.

Jon asked if there were any long-term side effects from

taking steroids, and Professor Straumberg gave him a look that turned me cold. Toby does not have a long term.

We were at Professor Straumberg's office for three days on that first visit. He has a little apartment above the medical centre where Jon and I stayed while Toby was downstairs being monitored.

Professor Straumberg wanted to get a long reading of the electrical activity in his brain. Toby had had EEGs before at our local hospital. They put a little rubber cap on his head with electrodes all over it. Graph paper gets fed through the EEG machine, and it draws a jagged line that shows all the spikes in brain activity. On these sheets, a seizure looks like a major earthquake, with the lines rushing to the top and bottom of the paper and filling the thing with black ink. But it's difficult to catch a seizure during a short EEG, unless the seizures are happening dozens of times a day.

The EEGs Toby had back in England were only about 20 minutes long. Professor Straumberg wanted to get a much longer reading, and more detailed, of both day and night-time activity. He glued about 30 electrodes directly onto Toby's scalp, in between the hair. The wires coming out of the electrodes fed into a little box about the size of an old walkman. It had a strap so Toby could walk around with it on. He hated the feeling of the electrodes and the glue in his hair. We had to keep telling him to leave them alone and not pick at them. He had to keep them on for 48 hours. Professor Straumberg hoped that he would have a seizure during that time so that he could get a good reading. It was odd to hope for and dread something at the same time.

In the end, Toby didn't have a seizure there. He had one on the boat on the way home. It was about ten at night and we had made a little bed for ourselves on the floor of the TV lounge with our coats. I was just dropping off when he started. It was panic stations as always. Lots of people were just standing there staring at us. And we didn't want help from the ones that wanted to help. A woman said we should put something in his mouth to stop him biting his tongue. It just shows how ignorant most people are about seizures.

If Toby's seizure caused any tremors on the boat, they were lost within the rumble of the engines. To everyone watching, the only unusual thing about this seizure was the length of it – 35 minutes, although to us this was short.

This experience on the boat made me terrified about a seizure happening in a public place. What if he had one in a café or a shop and the tremors were strong enough to shatter the front windows and they fell down on people? What if he hurt someone? It made me afraid to leave the house for a long while after we got back from Prague. I kept Toby out of school, which I think was a relief for them. After we'd first told them about his seizures, and the procedure that had to be followed if he had one, they looked petrified.

We put off contacting the Harrisons in Edinburgh for a long while. We just wanted to pretend that we were a normal family and that everything was okay. The last thing we wanted to do was talk to someone else about illness. The steroids and the new levels of medications that Professor Straumberg had put Toby on had reduced the number of seizures he was having to about three a month, and in between those seizures, we could pretend that everything was the way it used to be. But then one day I got a call from Melody Harrison, Nicholas's mother. Professor Straumberg had given her our details.

She and I clicked instantly. She was fighting to get a statement of special educational needs for Nicholas and was having a nightmare with it. Her local authority just kept turning her down, losing paperwork, not returning calls and writing letters quoting incorrect information. We were having *exactly* the same situation with Toby.

Sterna's episodes cause brain damage that affects short-term memory. It makes learning at school in a regular classroom setup impossible. As soon as information goes in, it gets scrambled. Toby can remember certain things with incredible accuracy, like if he's watching a TV show he really loves, he will have memorized the dialogue and the soundtrack and all the sound effects after watching it just two times. But if you sit him down and try to explain that two plus three equals five, it is just impossible for him.

The effects of Sterna's on short- and long-term memory is just one of the things that Professor Straumberg plans to research – please will you make a gift today of £25 to make it possible?

There were lots of other things that Melody and I had in common. It was actually wonderful to talk to her. So many people are like, 'Oh you poor thing, how do you cope?' Which just makes it worse. Melody and I had a good old moan about everything and I felt so much better afterwards. We arranged to meet a week later, during the Easter Holidays, in Liverpool, which was a half-way point between us.

The boys got on brilliantly. The brain damage caused by Sterna's means that the things they're interested in are a few years behind other children their age. Toby and Nicholas were both into the same TV shows, and Nicholas loved Toby's folder – it's an A4 ring binder filled with print outs of characters from his favourite TV shows. He carries it with him everywhere. It costs us a fortune in printer ink.

We just walked and walked, talking, Melody and me, all through the town and along the dock. It was so comforting to know I'm not alone.

Nicholas's seizures do not move objects, but affect the people around him. They create a feeling of intense fear. As if dealing with a seizure wasn't scary enough, when Melody looks after him, she experiences waves of dread and paranoia. She calls it the dark cloud. 'When the cloud comes,' she says all the time. She said she's had nurses in the hospital actually run away from the bedside during a seizure. She's the only one who can bear it.

One useful effect of Nicholas's cloud is that Melody can actually feel it coming on, so she gets a warning before the seizure starts. If they're together out in the car, or at the shops, she's got maybe a minute or two to get somewhere safe where she can deal with the seizure and call for help.

Professor Straumberg says no two Sterna's cases are the same. It's really an umbrella term for any seizure activity that affects anything outside of the body. The strength of the effect in different children varies greatly too. Some of them make Toby's seizures seem quite mild.

There was a little two-year-old boy in the Hague whose seizures caused severe nosebleeds in everyone within shouting distance.

No one knows why or how this type of epileptic seizure affects things outside of the child's body. Professor Straumberg says we may be decades away from an answer, but within the next year or two, within Toby's lifetime, Professor Straumberg's research could lead to better diagnosis and treatment.

It's vital that more is found out about Sterna's right now. Please will you help?

Professor Straumberg believes that Sterna's syndrome is caused by a recessive gene that only develops into full Sterna's when the mother and the father both have the gene and pass it to their male children – it only affects boys. It kills me that what Toby is going through might be my and Jon's fault. If we'd never met, or if we'd had a girl, we wouldn't know anything about Sterna's.

Professor Straumberg is trying to identify genetic markers in the parents of children with Sterna's. If he can find them, it will mean that within the next few years, a simple blood test can be used to diagnose Sterna's Syndrome before the symptoms even start to show. Professor Straumberg believes that something in the natural growth pattern of people with Sterna's causes these specific genes to 'switch on'. That's why the seizures always begin at about the same age – around six or seven. If he can find carriers of the Sterna's genes before their seizures have begun, he may be able to find a way to deactivate that switch. They would still carry the

Sterna's genes, but they would be inactive. This would, in effect, be a cure for Sterna's.

This is just one part of Professor Straumberg's research that he needs funding for.

He is also working with the Epilepsy Centre in Washington to build a global database of epilepsy sufferers as soon as they are diagnosed. He hopes that in this way, he may discover more carriers of Sterna's. With more people to include in his studies, the more he will be able to learn about it.

The final part of Professor Straumberg's research is to help people like Toby whose Sterna's episodes have already begun. The 'recipe' of medications that he put Toby on has already reduced the number of seizures by 60 percent. Professor Straumberg needs funding to do more research into the effects of combining medications. At the moment, prescribing the different medicines is a process of trial and error, moving the levels of one up and one down, substituting one drug for another and monitoring its effects till the right balance is reached. But it takes weeks for some of the drugs to take full effect. This means that finding the right dosages usually takes anywhere between six months and two years. To complicate this further, the child's body can build up a tolerance to some of the drugs, and the amounts required change as the child gets older and bigger. Professor Straumberg believes that with more funding and more study of the way drugs interact in the body, it will be possible to create a mathematical formula for prescribing anti-epileptics. This formula would mean that any consultant in any hospital could take a few body measurements from a patient and quickly calculate the exact amount necessary to control their seizures. It would mean an end to trial and error, giving the child maximum protection from seizures as quickly as possible.

Even though Toby is one of only a few Sterna's carriers in the world, the results of Professor Straumberg's research could mean dramatic improvements for people with all forms of hard to control epilepsy. Studying seizure activity at the most extreme end of the spectrum means that his research raises the level of knowledge about all other seizure types. At the moment, there are 600,000 people with epilepsy in the UK alone (that's one in every 103). It could mean a better quality of life for every one of them.

It's been 18 months since Toby's first seizure, and even though he's only having two or three a month, Jon and I are always on red alert. We have a baby monitor set up in his room, and a movement detector under his mattress, so if he starts to have a seizure we know about it immediately. But the alarm goes off sometimes when he just turns over, so almost every day the beeping wakes us up in the middle of the night and we go rushing into his room to see if he's okay. It's draining, that perpetual worry.

But we're not worrying about nothing.

Last week, Melody, Nicholas's mum called. She made a little sniff sound, and I knew right away that something was very wrong. She said, 'He's gone,' and then she broke down, and couldn't speak any more.

Melody called back the next day. She said the paramedics came but they couldn't stop Nicholas's seizure. It lasted 90 minutes. They couldn't stop it at home, or in the ambulance, and even at the hospital when they put the drip in, he was still going. They put as much medication into him as his body could take, but it still wasn't enough. His heart stopped, and he stopped breathing.

Sudden Unexpected Death in Epilepsy (SUDEP) causes about 500 deaths each year in the UK. SUDEP has taken every carrier of Sterna's Syndrome before they reach 13.

Nicholas was so little. He was only a year older than Toby. I'm so scared.

That's why I'm writing to you today. Toby's only hope is Professor Straumberg's research. There's a chance that Toby may be able to experience life as a teenager and maybe even an adult, but only if you can help.

I know you don't know me. Your name came on a list of people who have given to children's charities in the past. Maybe you give because a child close to you has been affected by an illness. Maybe you can understand what Toby, Jon and I are going through.

Please will you help save Toby's life with a gift of £25 today? Please. Professor Straumberg's research relies on the generous donations of people like you. I'm so scared of losing this opportunity. It might be the last chance we get.

Yours in hope.

Amy Colkiss
(Toby's mum)

Acknowledgements

Oh boy, there are so many people who've had a hand in putting this book in your hands, and I'm so grateful to them all.

The Arts Foundation awarded me the Arts Foundation Fellowship in Short Story Writing in 2011, which allowed me to quit my day job and write full-time for six months to finish this collection. Thanks to Shelley Warren and everyone at the Arts Foundation, to the judges: Alex Linklater, Kamila Shamsie, and Deborah Rogers, and thank you to the two short story champions who nominated me for this fellowship: Diana Reich from the Small Wonder Festival at Charleston, and Ra Page from Comma Press.

Thank you to all at the Sunday Times EFG Short Story Award and Booktrust – especially Cathy Galvin and Claire Shanahan, for shortlisting 'Fewer Things' in the inaugural year of this epic award and bringing my story to so many readers.

Thank you to AJ Ashworth, who asked me to contribute something to *Matter* Issue 9. I wrote the story 'Dead Fish Don't Blink,' which was the first, and almost identical, version of the story 'Dead Fish' in this collection.

Thank you to Ra Page (I'm not done thanking you yet, sir) at Comma Press for commissioning three of the stories in this collection for brilliantly themed anthologies: 'Tamagotchi' was for *The New Uncanny* – a collection of stories responding to Freud's essay on the uncanny; 'Without a Shell' was for *When it Changed* – real science fiction stories, based upon current scientific research (thanks also to Geoff Ryman who edited this book, and to Dr Vinod Dhanak who bought me lunch and blew my mind with tales about how nanotechnology is going to change the world); and 'An Industrial Evolution', which was for *Bio-Punk* – stories about the potential ethical consequences of current biotechnology research (thanks also to Professor Bruce Whitelaw at the Roslin Institute in Edinburgh, home of Dolly the sheep, who bought me coffee and showed me the picture of bioluminescent piglets that he has on his desk, and thanks to Dr Jan Deckers at Newcastle University for his sound ethical advice).

Thanks to Jim Hinks and Katie Slade at Comma – you guys are the best.

Thanks to Robin D Laws and Simon Rogers from Stone Skin Press for asking me to contribute to *The New Hero* anthology – 'The Captain' was my answer to their brief, after many months of creating superheroes and chucking them in the bin.

Thanks to my family and friends for their support, encouragement, and comforting throughout, especially Alison MacLeod, Rob Shearman, Wena Poon and Clare Wigfall.

Big love to Will Francis, my agent at Janklow and Nesbit, Ra Page, my editor at Comma Press, and Naomi, my wife at home – all of whom care enough to tell me when I've produced something faulty, and who are kind enough to say lovely things when I've produced something that's worthy of you, the reader.

And finally, thank you to my boys, my delightful, mischievous little muses.

ALSO AVAILABLE FROM THIS AUTHOR....

Instruction Manual for Swallowing

Adam Marek

ISBN-13: 978 1905583041

Robotic insects, in-growing cutlery, flesh-serving waiters in a zombie cafe... Welcome to the surreal, misshapen universe of Adam Marek's first collection; a bestiary of hybrids from the techno-crazed future and mythical past; a users' guide to the seemingly obvious (and the world of illogic implicit within it). Whether fantastical or everyday in setting, Marek's stories lead us down to the engine room just beneath modern consciousness, a place of both atavism and familiarity, where the body is fluid, the spirit mechanised, and beasts often tell us more about our humanity than anything we can teach ourselves.

Praise for Adam Marek:

'Marek's fabulously meaty, funny writing makes the short story look really exciting again, pulling you, frame by frame, into a bright, strange future.'
– Maggie Gee

'There's a transgressive thrill to Adam Marek's debut collection of short stories that's not simply a result of the potency of the subject matter... delightful.'
- *The Guardian*

'Early McEwan meets David Cronenberg.... genuine, unsettling talent'
- *The Independent*

'Marek is terrific at setting an off-kilter mood.'
- *The National Post*